Mine to Adore

Veteran K9 Team

Book 4

Kameron Claire

Snuggle Whore Press, LLC

Dedication

This series is dedicated to every individual
who signs a blank check on their ass
by enlisting in the Armed Forces
to serve their country—and to the
loved ones who support them back home.

We are Witty, Wicked & Wild wherever we go!

VETERAN
K9
TEAM
REPORTING
FOR DUTY

Chapter One
Linc

Wiping the sleep out of my eyes, I grab Li-Lou and follow Barron and Sarge from the parking lot into the Silver Mountain Ski Lodge. Barron brought me out here at the end of last season—one week after I ETS'd and moved to Colorado—and introduced me to the Search and Rescue supervisor, Brad Schmidt. One test run down the mountain followed by a couple of beers while telling old Army stories and Schmidt hired me even though there are dozens on a waitlist that goes back a couple of years.

That pissed off a few of the old timers who have friends on said list.

It is also one of the many good things about being ex-Army. We have our own form of nepotism, and considering my Army brethren are the only family I've got, it's the only patronage I'm going to get. I worked every weekend with Barron for the rest of February and March until the resort closed down and will work every other weekend up here this season until I'm too old to ski.

Like Barron says, once you get on the payroll, you don't give up your position. Ever.

Considering I have no desire to go back to Arkansas for the holidays, I'll volunteer for every extra shift I can get my hands on, too.

It's not like I have anything else going on, and I need the money.

We walk through the rental area to the staff door. While Barron pulls out his phone to find the security code, I glance around the room, my gaze instantly going to a couple of hot blondes trying on rental boots. The women are giggling, and there is something so bewitching about them in this moment that I go tunnel vision. The one sitting down is cute with her strawberry blonde braids, but it's the platinum blonde kneeling in front of her that I can't seem to take my eyes off of. Maybe it's the pure moment between the two of them right now—like they don't have a care in the world. Their joy is infectious, but it's the lyrical teasing of the one on her knees that has me entranced.

Or maybe it's her dark eyes, cute button nose, and full-lipped smile.

I wonder if they are friends or sisters?

Either way, two of them and two of us. Perfect.

"Holy shit," I hiss to keep my voice low enough that only Barron will hear. "Do you think they're sisters?"

Barron glances over his shoulder in their direction. "Don't know. Why?"

"We should ask them out," I say with absolute surety, positive he will glom onto my brilliant idea.

He punches in the code, and the door pops open. "No."

The finality of his one spoken word has me snapping my eyes to him. "Why not?"

"Sweet Jesus. To be a young horndog full of self-confidence again," he grumbles, leading the way inside the restricted staff area.

Horndog—I hate being called that, even if there was a time when there was a semblance of truth to it. I'm a natural born flirt. It's one of the survival mechanisms I learned from my mother, but the negative connotation that accompanies *horndog* has always bothered me.

It's right up there with slut, manwhore, and douchebag—none of which I want to be known as.

Not anymore.

I follow behind Barron and hold the door open with my back as I stand in the threshold and stare at them. "One, I'm not a horndog, but fully aware of what I like—and blondes with beautiful smiles do it for me. Secondly, when's the last time you had sex? And thirdly, what's the harm in asking them out?"

Barron glances out at the women. "You might not be a horndog today, but I've known you since you were nineteen years old, so don't act like you've always been sweet and innocent. Secondly, my sex life is none of your business and you better never ask me about it again. And lastly, we can't date them. It's part of our employment contract that we don't ask out the resort guests."

That breaks me out of my trance, and my eyes snap back to his. "Really? I agreed to that crap?"

He shrugs. "It's a fraternization thing."

Well, fuck me.

I was so excited about the job that I read none of the fine print. Not that it doesn't make sense, but it's not what I want to hear at this moment. I've been out of the military and living in Colorado for ten months now, and in that time, I've only dated one woman for a couple of months.

Which is why I was defensive when he called me a horndog. My days of chasing tail have been over for quite some time, but I can't seem to shed my manwhore veneer. "Fine. If we see them on Sunday after we get off work, we'll ask them out."

"And then what?" He shakes his head. "They're renting their equipment, which means they're not local. They're probably flying back to Southern California or Florida or some other beachfront property next week."

"Man." I give up my post at the door and push past Barron into the locker room. "You're bumming me out."

He walks into the office and grabs our dorm keys off a peg board. "You're better off finding a woman in Spring City if a relationship is what you're looking for."

Sighing, I throw my jacket with the rest of my gear into the locker they assigned me two weeks ago. "I don't know what I'm looking for, man. I figure when I find it, I'll know."

Barron looks at me with a hint of amusement and

nods. "Maybe you'll be lucky, and it'll smack you upside the head with a two-by-four."

I raise my brow. Barron was married when I started working for him and in the middle of a divorce when I got back from my first deployment. I really know nothing about his relationship, considering he isn't the kind of man to talk about his personal life—especially not back then when I was his subordinate. "Is that how it was for you?"

Frowning, he shakes his head. "No. I don't think everyone gets a lightning bolt. I certainly never did."

Something about his tone tells me to drop the subject, even though I would love nothing more than to have a male role model to talk about relationships with. Although, maybe Barron isn't the right guy, even with thirteen years of experience on me. Vale, on the other hand, is head over heels in love with his new bride. Maybe he's got a few pointers for me.

We grab a bite at the grille before getting our dogs settled in our dorm room for the night. The accommodations are not bad considering they are free, but not much bigger than the barracks we lived in at Fort Lewis. They are considerably nicer than the tents or connex we shack up in while deployed, so I'm thankful no matter what.

I lie on my twin bed as something plays on the television, but I'm not really paying attention to the movie. My mind is on the pretty blonde from the rental shop.

I wonder where she is staying tonight?

Barron said they aren't local and we'll probably never see them again, which makes sense, I guess. And yet my brain, heart, and dick are scheming a way to run into her tomorrow so I can introduce myself.

If I can finagle twenty minutes with her, I know I can charm her into having dinner with me.

And then, who knows?

VETERAN
K9
TEAM
REPORTING
FOR DUTY

Chapter Two
Brandi

Days away from my fortieth birthday, I wake up in a million-dollar house overlooking a posh Colorado ski resort courtesy of my beautiful and generous daughter.

A few months ago, she landed her dream job and moved from our Arizona home to Spring City, Colorado. This job is going to set her up for way more than I could provide for her in her youth.

I couldn't be prouder of her.

She's never skied before. We couldn't afford it when she was growing up, but I used to ski a lot when I was a kid, and I am thrilled to be hitting the slopes this morning.

"Good morning, sweetheart." I poke my head into my daughter's bedroom—the one she claimed in this gorgeous VRBO—and find her bed empty.

I am seventeen years and three months older than

Betty, and if you do the math, that means I got pregnant with her when I was sixteen and a half.

I was young and thought I was in love.

David—or the sperm donor, as Betty calls him—also thought he was in love, or so he said. We did not discuss things like love and passion in our ultraconservative religious homes in northern Utah. Marriage and responsibility were topics at the dinner table, as were service and duty (and don't forget devotion and worship), but never love or passion—or god forbid, sex. It's no wonder the redheaded boy from the family down the road swept me off my feet by paying attention to me in a way that no one else ever had.

I would've followed him to the ends of the earth back then.

After we found out I was pregnant, my family lost their minds and the options they gave me were not good. They wanted to send me away to a home for pregnant teenagers and give my child away before I ever held her. Only then—if I saved my family from shame—would I be allowed to come home.

David whisked me away from there, a knight-in-shining-armor to my damsel-in-distress. He promised to be the only answer I would ever need and my teenage brain believed him.

So, we high-tailed it across the high desert to the Valley of the Sun.

Even as my belly grew, my life felt like a fairytale until the day I gave birth. On that day, my knight in shining armor took one look at our beautiful baby girl and said, *I can't do this.* I suppose the reality of standing face to face with his child made him rethink the love and devotion he once told me was mine to have forever.

Honestly, I can't understand it because one look at Betty's little cherub face and I knew what true love felt like.

Not that any of that matters anymore.

Nothing I went through has ever made me regret having my beautiful daughter here with me today. She's perfect, and she's not only my child but also my best friend. Many people think we're sisters. Maybe it's because I look young for my age, but I think it's because our personalities are so much alike.

Walking downstairs, I find her curled up on the cushions in the big bay window overlooking the ski resort with her phone in her hand.

Ugh! That girl always has her phone in her hand.

Then I notice the skies outside are gray and dreary compared to the crystal blue ones we drove under yesterday. "What happened to the clear skies?"

Betty looks up from her phone and sighs. "I told you, they say if you don't like the weather, wait five minutes."

I giggle. "I thought you hate it when they say that."

"I do. It's obnoxious."

"But is it true?" I take her cup of coffee out of her hand and take a sip.

Frowning, she snatches her mug back. As an only child—considering I did not give her a lot because I couldn't afford to splurge—she isn't much on sharing. "Probably."

"Are we risking the slopes this morning?" I check her with my hip and force her to scoot over so I can sit next to her.

Her frown deepens. She's never been on skis one day in her life, and the only reason we are here is because of my birthday. "Well, I have my ski lesson at eleven and I can't come up with a good reason to cancel."

"Good. The sooner you learn how to ski, the sooner we'll be hitting the slopes together. I'll get changed." I kiss her cheek and jump up, energized about the day.

When I was a kid, I skied every winter, and I was quite good, but it's been twenty-four years since I could afford to go. For an Arizona girl, a ski weekend is an investment and we've never had the disposable income.

I bounce up the stairs two at a time and quickly change into my new ski outfit, courtesy of my amazing daughter and her high-roller six-figure income.

Have I mentioned how proud I am?

Ten minutes later, I come downstairs to find Betty standing up from her perch in the window. "Hurry. Your lesson may not be until eleven, but we can use the time at the lodge to see what kind of yummies they have on the menu for later."

"Your sweet tooth and my ass need to break up." She rolls her eyes and sets her coffee cup in the kitchen sink.

I smack said behind. "Sweetheart, there's nothing wrong with your ass. I could bounce a quarter off of your butt."

"Well, I'm glad you think so, because something tells me I'm going to be on it a lot today."

"Pish posh." I wave her concerns away. "A couple of lessons and you'll be skiing with me in no time."

"We can hope."

Finally, twenty minutes later, we're walking into the lodge, carrying our rented gear.

Betty grumbles beside me. "I think I have too many clothes on."

"You'll be fi—" I take one look at her red face and try to suppress my smile "—ohhh… maybe you can take off your jacket and stuff it in the locker if you get hot."

She looks up at the gray skies that seem to get darker as the morning creeps toward noon. "You know, maybe you should get a couple of runs in now. We may not have all afternoon to ski."

I nod. "I was thinking the same thing. Are you sure you'll be okay by yourself?"

She chuckles. "Mom, I'm twenty-three years old and completely capable of ignoring people by scrolling TikTok on my phone while sitting near the fire in a ski lodge—similar to what I would do at a coffee shop in Spring City."

Frowning, I shake my head. She does always have her head in that damn phone. Of course, it's also why she now has a six-figure income, so I guess I shouldn't complain. But I want her to make friends and meet somebody and she can't do that if she's never making eye contact. "We need to work on your social skills."

Her mouth falls open. "Who are you talking to?"

Chuckling, I hold up my hands and nod. "Okay. We need to work on *our* social skills. I'm going to get on the lift and tackle this mountain. I will see you in forty-five minutes."

"Sounds perfect. Have fun."

"You know I will." I wave over my head as I walk towards the first lift.

Ski resorts have gotten high tech since the last time I skied. Everything from the ticketing system, to the lifts, to the choose-your-own-adventure trails has me turned around. But I figure in the end, all hills come down to the same spot, so I'll take this baby to the top and get the ride of my life done before it gets too nasty out to ski.

The farther up I ride, the fewer skiers are waiting to board the lift.

Honestly, I should've taken that as my first clue.

When I get to the tippy top of Silver Mountain, the guy running the lift yells, "This is the last run of the day! Make sure you get down to the lodge in a safe but reasonable time!"

That should've been my second clue.

Visibility isn't great, but it isn't horrible either—although it is obvious a storm is coming in—so I push off and head down what I think is the main trail. A giant gust of air, stronger than the wind already blowing, smacks me in the side of my head, knocking my body off balance and lifting my new knit hat off my head. I stay on my feet, but I'm heading into the trees—and how the hell did I end up in the trees?

I miss one giant trunk, turning sharply to miss a second one, when my foot hits a divot and the tip of my ski plows into a soft bank of slushy snow. Next thing I know, I'm flying through the air, one binding giving while the other one doesn't.

My body is in motion, twisting to the right while a tree holds my ski hostage. The binding finally gives, and I'm thrown into a large snowdrift, my knee instantly throbbing in pain.

At first, I can focus on nothing but the pain as it courses through my body, but as it subsides, I glance around, surrounded by trees and fluffy snow.

I take stock of my body. At least I wasn't knocked unconscious or thrown head-first into a tree. As it is, I'm propped up against one, my soft skull barely avoiding a horrific accident.

I try to stand up but sink thigh-deep into a drift of soft snow not tamped down by hundreds of avid skiers.

How the hell did I fall so far from the trail?

The wind howls, the sound deafening, but at least in the trees I'm protected from the storm's onslaught.

I swear the temperature has dropped another ten degrees in the last few minutes.

I can't wait to tell Betty—Coloradans aren't kidding when they say to wait five minutes.

Crawling on top of the snow to avoid sinking deep, I find one broken ski, the other lost to oblivion. Staying low seems to be my best defense, but without two functioning skis, how the hell am I going to get back to the lodge?

How is anyone going to find me in this?

Minutes ago, I wasn't alone, but now?

I feel like the only person on the mountain.

I reach for my phone, but my arms don't want to work. I'm freezing, bundled up tight, unable to make my limbs move away from my core. At some point, I drew the hood of my thick coat tight around my head, but I don't remember putting it on. In my fight to survive, I've done things I don't recall.

My knee no longer throbs. Actually, I can't feel my knee, or my feet, fingers, or nose and I'm wondering how long I've been out here.

Oh my god! Am I going to die out here?

VETERAN
K9
TEAM
REPORTING
FOR DUTY

Chapter Three
Linc

Where is she?

Where the fuck is she?

I radio in and talk to the guy who had been running Glacier Point Peak, the last stop of the lifts. "Did you see a female skier wearing a black and neon jacket with a neon yellow and pink hat?"

Thank god I saw her right before she got on the lifts, but unfortunately it's a clearance jacket from last year's retro line and there were a dozen or more on the slopes today. The hat, however, is all her.

"Yeah, she was one of the last people off before we shut down. I told her to head down immediately since there would be no more runs for the day."

"You didn't think you should ski down behind her and make sure she got to the lodge in one piece?" I clench my fist.

He's lucky we aren't face-to-face right now.

"Uh, no man. I rode the lift down with Tyler."

Stupid motherfucking teenagers! I hate working with them. They don't think things through.

"Why? Is she okay?"

"No! She's missing, you stupid ass. You're supposed to help ensure people get off the mountain when shutting down a lift. Do you have anything helpful to tell me while I look for her?"

I am met with dead silence.

Fuck! I scream into the howling wind. Dispatch already checked the video feed, which has been useless for the last fifteen minutes due to near white-out conditions near the top of the mountain.

Li-Lou, my search and rescue-trained Husky with hardened military experience, whimpers next to me. She's strapped into the sidecar on my snowmobile via a waterproof lining and she's sensitive to the anxiety rising in my chest.

I glance over and rub the top of her head, the only part exposed. "We have to find her."

Li-Lou whimpers again and nudges my hand as if to say, "Let's go."

I climb back to the top of the mountain; the wind wiping away any useful tracks. The near blinding snow is quickly eradicating even my own tracks.

But then I see it. A lone ski half-buried with no skier attached.

"You ready to earn your kibble?" I pull the bungee cord and release the waterproof lining covering both of us. Li-Lou hops out of the sidecar, instantly running into the trees beyond the trail on the backside of the mountain.

I follow, nudging the snowmobile in as far as I can until the trees get too dense. Li-Lou howls and I jump off the mobile, grabbing my emergency pack and running in her direction.

"That's my girl!" I exclaim, diving to my knees next to Brandi, who's propped up against a tree, curled into herself.

She's not moving, even though Li-Lou is nudging with her nose and pawing at her leg.

"Brandi? Can you hear me?" I lift her chin gently to see her face, uncertain of any trauma done to her neck and head. She has on goggles, but the puff of hot breath hitting the frigid air lets me know she's alive.

"Brandi?"

"So cold," she murmurs.

Shit. I can't assess her out here for injury, but Ranger Station Twelve is only a quarter of a mile from here.

"I'm picking you up." Scooping her into my arms, I trudge out of the thick, spongy snow back to the snowmobile. I should have put her on a sled, as the physical exertion of plodding through the snow has me sweating and breathing hard, but at this moment, the only thing I care about is pulling us out of the blizzard and getting her warm and dry.

I put her in the sidecar and jump in the driver's seat, patting my leg for Li-Lou to jump up. We won't be going fast and she has amazing balance. A couple minutes later,

I'm parked under an overhang. I enter a code—praying it is the same as the secure areas down in the lodge—and push open the door to a decently stocked station mostly maintained in the summer as an emergency firefighter station.

I lift her into my arms again and carry her inside. There's a wood pellet heater in the corner and a big hearth in the middle of one wall. Setting her down on the floor in front of the fireplace, I make quick work of lighting both fires and run back outside to grab my go bag and throw a tarp over the snowmobile.

Kneeling down next to her, I pull off my gloves and gently loosen the drawstring holding her hood tight over her head. Her blonde hair spills out, none of which is red or sticky.

Thank god. No head trauma.

"Brandi?" I say again, needing her to maintain consciousness.

Her eyes flutter open. "Cold."

"I know. I have the fires going, but we need to get you out of these wet clothes before hypothermia sets in. And I need to assess you for frostbite."

She groans. "Too cold for frostbite."

I grin. She's sassy, which, to me, is a fantastic sign of her overall health.

"I'm trying to warm you up, but you're not being very cooperative."

She opens her eyes fully, big brown orbs reflecting the flames from the fireplace. "How am I being uncooperative?"

"You're not letting me get you naked." I smile, smoothing her hair back from her face.

She chuckles and slowly moves her arms, unfurling from her protective state. "You and no other men."

"No other men what?" I ask, needing to keep her talking and her brain engaged. Unzipping her coat as she unwraps her arms from her core, I'm thankful to find her unscathed.

Frozen, but otherwise unharmed, from what I can tell. By my estimate, she's been exposed for fifteen to twenty minutes—a lifetime in the middle of a blizzard.

"No other men—" she drags in a ragged breath "—trying to get me naked."

"Oh, I doubt that. You're sexy when you're tinted blue and covered in snow. It can only get better from here." With immense care, I pull off her gloves, her fingers frozen and stiff. She might have the beginning stages of frostbite, but nothing that can't be reversed.

Snatching my pack, I dump it on the floor and pull off my jacket. I grab a hand warmer, crack it and slide it inside a glove, handing it back to her and clasping her bare hands around it. "Hold on to this. It should be hot in seconds."

After some careful prodding, I sit her up with her back to the sofa. She winces as she drags her legs out in front of her.

"What hurts?"

"My knee." She glances at her left leg.

"Okay, first we'll get your coat off, then we'll work on your pants."

"Aren't you going to buy me a drink first?"

My head snaps up to see a playful smile spreading her blue-tinted lips.

"I'll buy you whatever you want if you help me get this off." I tug on her sleeve.

She drops the glove in her lap and leans forward. I pull her jacket off and toss it aside, then pop the suspenders on the ski bib pants she's wearing. Her clothes are new, but her boots are rented, which makes me wonder what the hell she was doing at the top of the mountain. People at that level own their equipment.

I move down and pop the bindings on her boots, loosening them as much as possible. If her knee is twisted, yanking this off is going to hurt like hell.

She sighs and I'm assuming it feels good to relieve the pressure of the hard cast boots.

"I need to pull this off, but I don't want to hurt you anymore than I have to." Positioning her hands below her knee, I hope to have her stabilize herself to the best of her ability. "Can you do me a favor and put your hands right here?"

She drops the glove again, her fingers slowly gaining some color, and wraps her hands around the base of her knee.

"Okay, Brandi, hold your breath."

She inhales deeply and tightens her jaw, her eyes glued to mine as I wiggle the boot until it is as close as I can get and then pull with a quick sharp tug.

She hisses, winces and then nods her head. "That wasn't too bad."

"Good." I pull off her other boot and then her pants as she lifts her hips for me.

"Keep talking to me, Brandi. Let me know you don't have brain freeze." I throw her a flirty wink.

"How do you know my name?" She shivers despite the roaring fire in front of her.

"I met your daughter on the bunny hill."

"She's going to be a mess when I don't come back."

I smile to myself, thinking about Barron. Even though he tried to act unaffected yesterday, I saw his eyes flash with interest when we saw the women in the lodge again this morning. Of course, I wanted to talk to them, but he silently shook his head and glanced down at his phone with his ski instructor list for the morning, dismissing my idea. Imagine my surprise to find him on the bunny hill with one of them when we got the order to shut down the mountain. "My partner, her instructor, is hanging out with her until we call in. Once we get you warm, we can let her know you are okay."

I pull a thermal blanket out of my pack, unfold it and wrap it around her. She has cold-weather underwear on —which for now I'll let her keep—but even with it, I can tell her left knee is almost twice the size of the right.

Standing up, I shed my outerwear, my underclothes soaked with sweat. Shit, I need to get undressed too, but I need to get her naked and under a dozen blankets first.

I crouch down next to Brandi again. "Hey, I know I was teasing earlier about getting you naked, but I actually need to get you out of your wet clothes."

"Where's my drink?" she jokes through chattering

teeth while simultaneously lifting her arms over her head.

I smile. "I promise not only will I buy you drinks, I'll buy you dinner if you get naked and under these blankets."

"I'm a nurse. I understand the drill."

"You're a nurse? Why didn't you say so?" I pull off her shirt.

"I like you taking care of me." Without asking, I unhook her bra with nimble fingers. She giggles, or what I can only assume is a giggle. Her jaw is moving at mach ten, which is a good thing, while her body tries to warm up. "You've got the skills of a twenty-year-old with lots of practice."

I pull the thermal blanket tight around her, tying the ends into a toga over her shoulder, shielding her breasts from my view.

Not that I didn't peek.

"I wouldn't say I have that much practice." Grabbing the blanket from the couch, I throw it over her lap. I already know I want to get naked with this woman—I knew it the moment I saw her—but this is not the way I want to do it.

I had envisioned more of a striptease scenario.

Yes, my imagination is that filthy.

"I'm sure you've had more practice than me."

"What are you telling me? Are you a virgin? Is that daughter I met on the ski slopes an immaculate concep-tion kind of deal?" I waggle my brows, teasing her as I slide my hands under the blanket and tug on the tops of her leggings. "Lift your hips again."

She does, although I can tell the movement is taxing for her. Exhausted from the exposure, I need to get her warm and only then can I let her sleep.

"I'm not a virgin," she says.

"Good. Virgins make me twitchy." I wink and stand up. "I'll be right back."

In the back bedroom, I find one pair of men's sweatpants—mountain issue and one size too small—and a stack of blankets. I shed my thermals, my balls shriveled up tight against the cold fabric and don the sweatpants. Thankfully, I also find a couple pairs of wool socks.

Carrying them back to the living room, I find Brandi sitting upright with her eyes closed.

"Open up your eyes, beautiful. I need you to stay awake a little longer." I pick her up and set her lengthwise on the couch before piling blankets on top of her and sliding dry socks on her feet.

Her eyes open slowly, but then bug out as they land on me. "Holy hell."

I glance down at my inked chest and then back up. "The tattoos?"

"The muscle."

"I can make them dance for you, if you like."

"What else can you make dance?"

Her flirty banter and suggestive comments have my blood rushing, and considering I'm wearing sweatpants with no support, my youthful exuberance is about to be very apparent if I don't get my mind back on the job.

Shit. Maybe I'll be the one to perform a striptease?

VETERAN
K9
TEAM

REPORTING
FOR DUTY

Chapter Four
Brandi

I'm as comfortable as I can be given the situation and yet even with the fire and a mountain of blankets, I'm freezing.

Meanwhile, Hot Stuff is running around shirtless in low-slung gray sweatpants—the epitome of men's lingerie. If looking at him doesn't heat me up from the inside, nothing will.

He stuffs a pillow under my knee to prop it up and then casts me a concerned look as I continue to chatter my teeth. "I'm going to make you something warm to drink."

"Whiskey?"

"Maybe later, if there's any here, but for now, it's hot cocoa. You need the sugar." He cups my face and strokes his thumb along my cheek for a moment before jumping up.

Walking into the kitchenette, he rummages around

the cupboards while I watch. "Keep those eyes open, sexy."

"I'm watching your muscles flex as you move," I murmur, my eyes half-closed.

Holy hell, why did I say that out loud? I don't talk to men like that, but my brain doesn't seem capable of filtering my thoughts before they form words and fly out of my mouth. What else have I said in the last however many minutes?

"What time is it?"

"It's about one. Why? You got a hot date or something?" He walks toward me with a steamy mug of hot cocoa.

"No one hotter than you."

Again? Now I'm really worried about what I said before my brain started functioning.

He sits next to me on the couch and offers me the mug to take a sip. He buried my hands under twenty pounds of fabric, so I have no choice but to accept his help like an invalid.

"Are you not cold?" I look pointedly at his wide chest.

Good god, it's like the gods carved him from stone.

"I couldn't find a sweatshirt in the bedroom, but as soon as you're settled, I'll wrap up in a blanket."

"You could get under the blankets with me."

Yep, that just came out of my mouth.

"I think your blood sugar is low, because there's no way I'm lucky enough to be hit on by a woman like you."

He offers me another sip and then another until my teeth stop chattering. "Feeling better?"

Nodding, I smile. "Thank you."

"It's my job, but also my pleasure."

"I could've died out there," I say without the full impact of my situation weighing down on me. If I took the time to think about it, I'd be freaking out right now.

"Yeah, but I wasn't going to let that happen."

Suddenly, there's a nose pushing and prodding through all the blankets. I look down to see a beautiful Husky with bright blue eyes. "Who is this?"

"This is my baby, Li-Lou. To be fair, she's the one who actually found you."

"Hi, sweet girl. If I had a treat, I'd give it to you."

My mystery man—whose name I now realize I don't know—slides his hand over my hip, tucking the blankets under my ass. "Think you're up for a phone call?"

"Yes, but I don't want to alarm my daughter, so we're going to pretend like everything was nice and simple. Maybe you should tell me your name?"

"My name's Lincoln, but my friends call me Linc."

"Is that your first or your last name?"

"Funny enough, it's my first name."

"What's your last name, Lincoln?"

"You wouldn't believe me if I told you."

"Try me."

"Abrams."

My mouth falls open. "You're kidding me. Your parents did that to you on purpose?"

He smiles. "Yeah."

"Well, thank you, Lincoln Abrams and Li-Lou, for rescuing me." I smile as he offers me another sip of cocoa. The sweet liquid has cooled and I take a bigger sip, predictably dribbling some on my chin. Linc is on it though, swiping it off with his thumb, which he then sucks into his mouth. It is the hottest thing a man has ever done to and for me, which tells you how low my bar for men is.

His eyes sparkle, and he hooks his finger under my chin, closing my slack jaw. Then he picks up a radio, clicks a button and doesn't say another word to me.

"Barron?"

Two seconds later, another male's voice comes over the line. "I read you."

"I got her, but I don't think we're going to make it down the mountain."

"Why? What's going on?"

My eyes grow wide, and Linc soothes my concerns with a gentle pat on my thigh. "She's fine. She's right here—"

Linc puts his hand over the mouthpiece and says, "Betty's with my partner. Let her know you're okay."

I speak aloud, trying to keep my voice calm. "Betty?"

"Mom? Are you okay?" My daughter sounds frantic, so I do my best to come across as calm as possible.

"I'm fine. Pissed, but I'm fine."

"What happened to you?"

I growl and roll my eyes. "Short story: I overestimated my abilities, went to the top of the lifts, got turned around in the blizzard and ended up on the backside of the mountain."

Linc cuts in. "We're at Ranger Station Twelve."

The male voice returns. "And you guys can't make it down the mountain?"

"Possibly could, but I don't want to risk it," Linc says.

"Any medical needs?" he replies.

"Negative." Linc's eyes travel over my body, as if he still has concerns.

"I'm sorry for ruining our game night." I blurt.

"It's fine, Mom. We can play tomorrow."

Linc responds. "Conditions are near white out up here and according to dispatch, the weather is only going to get worse over the next couple of hours. I got a fire going and basic provisions on me, so we'll be good until the morning."

"Okay. I'll keep the line open in case you need me."

"Roger. We'll be fine." Linc depresses the button and sets the radio down. "How was that?"

"Perfect. Do you think she'll be okay down there?"

"My partner, the man with her, his name is Barron. He escorted your daughter back to the house to look for you and I'm sure if she wants his company, he'll hang out with her for as long as she likes."

Linc stands up, opens a closet door and grabs an expandable drying rack. Then he grabs all our clothes off the floor, hanging them to dry. "I'm afraid you're going to have to stay naked until these clothes dry."

"I'm snug as a bug underneath the blankets, but you

look like you're cold." I glance pointedly at his rock-hard nipples.

"It's a little nippily." He grabs a blanket and wraps it around his neck, letting it drape over his chest, obscuring my view. "Body heat is better, but I guess this will have to do for now."

"The offer to snuggle with me is still there, but now that we've called my daughter, I think I'd like to sleep for a bit."

He nods. "I guess that would be okay. How would you like to snuggle?"

I lift from my prone position and purposely look over my shoulder.

He doesn't say a word, smiling and taking a seat behind me. We both scoot forward and then he leans back on the pillows and pulls me back against his chest, wrapping his bulging biceps around me. His body is infinitely warmer than the couch cushions and it takes no time to fall asleep.

I wake up with soft breath caressing my neck, powerful arms wrapped around my torso and a huge hand covering my bare breast... and something hard poking my ass.

I blink a couple times, unsure of where I am, but it doesn't take long for it to come back to me.

I am safe.

I am warm.

And I'm alive.

I dare to move my head, which only causes the surrounding arms to tighten and the hand to flex its fingers.

Sweet Jesus, it's been forever since a man has touched me and it feels so good right now. It's a reminder that I'm alive—a flesh and blood woman with needs and desires that go unfulfilled more often than not.

I haven't spent the last twenty-three years sexless. I've had a couple of friends-with-benefits along the way, lasting anywhere from six months to a couple years. But I would never allow it to turn into more, and eventually the man would start a relationship with somebody they could have a future with and we would go our separate ways.

However, I don't know if it's because I'm a woman and I can't divorce sex from emotion, but none of those trysts ever satisfied me. They scratched an inch, sometimes a good itch, but that was it. I know Betty moved to Colorado to give me space. She wants me to find a man who will be everything I should've had with her father, and while I appreciate her thought process, I wonder if I'm too old to try.

Ugh. I have to pee and I have no idea how I'm going to extricate myself from this situation.

Or if I want to.

We are so cozy right now.

"How do you feel?" A deep voice reverberates in my

ear, but he doesn't move his hand, unapologetically holding onto my breast like a security blanket.

"I'm thirsty and I need to use the bathroom. I also have a slight headache, but otherwise I feel amazing."

"Yeah, we need to pump a bunch of water into you now that you've warmed up and some more sugary hot cocoa would be good, too. I also have energy bars, which would be good for your stomach. I can get those while you're using the bathroom."

"Uh, I think maybe you shouldn't stand up yet."

"Why? Because of my hard-on?" Linc chuckles. "I fell asleep with a beautiful naked woman in my arms. It was bound to happen."

"You're not self-conscious at all, are you?"

"Getting an erection is natural, but if it offends you, you're going to have to get up first and give me a minute without your body pressed against mine. Because I guarantee you, he will not go down with you lying on top of me."

Turning my face away from him, I bite my lip to hide my smile, a myriad of snarky comebacks dancing on the tip of my tongue. How easy it would be to roll over, slide down his body and greet him in the most carnal way.

But I have to pee.

I move to sit up and maneuver the mountain of blankets pinning me in place. He pulls his hands out and helps me push them down. "I'm not offended. Flattered, actually. Although I'm sure at your age, you get hard for pretty much anyone or any reason."

His hands grip my upper arms and he pulls me back

against him, his mouth at my ear. "Let's get one thing straight, Brandi. I noticed you yesterday at the ski shop and had full intentions of finding you today to ask you out. Fate dictated another situation for the two of us, but in the end we're together, which is exactly what I wanted, and I don't get hard for just anyone."

He flexes his fingers and rubs my arms. "Now, I had no intention of saying all of that to you, because we're stuck here together and if you're not interested, I will respect you. But don't dismiss my physical reaction to you, because I promise you—" he moves his hips to let me know exactly how hard he is "—inspired this."

Sucking in my breath, I sit frozen against him, unsure of what to say. I've never had a man be so bold, forward and blatantly honest with me.

It's unbelievably hot.

He grabs a handful of blankets and flings them over the back of the couch, leaving me with the thermal blanket draped loosely over my shoulder—one boob hanging out. He adjusts it, tucking my boob back into hiding and smacking my thigh gently. "Go use the bathroom and I'll get everything else situated."

"Okay."

I move my legs out and am immediately reminded of my twisted knee. Hissing, I clutch at my swollen knee and hoist it up, swinging it over the edge.

Linc springs up from behind me, nimble as a cat and crouches in front of me. "Yeah, we'll need to wrap that up in ice."

He swings me into his arms before I can protest,

lifting me off the couch. "Until then, I'll have to carry you."

I settle into the warmth of his body and the strength of his arms. "You better be careful, Linc. A woman could get used to this."

"You should be used to a man moving heaven and hell to take care of you. Physically, emotionally, spiritually—" his hazel eyes sparkle "—sexually."

Oh my. I might take him up on that last part.

VETERAN
K9
TEAM
REPORTING
FOR DUTY

Chapter Five
Linc

I should not be flirting with the woman stranded with me in a mountain cabin. They'll definitely kick me off the Search and Rescue team if she complains and yet, I can't help myself.

I wanted her the minute I saw her, even more so now. She is smart, even sexier up close and now that I've held her naked body in my arms... forget about it.

I couldn't stop the blatant come-ons if my life depended upon it.

I check in with dispatch. They say to expect another three to four inches in the next two hours and then it should calm down. Doesn't matter, we're definitely staying the night here, but how will we occupy our time?

Fuck, I'm definitely going to hell.

Arrrraarrrooooo.

I look down at Li-Lou, who is making it known she's hungry and demands to be fed.

"Time for kibble, girl?"

Arrroooo.

"Do you think so? Well, we don't have any steak, so you're going to have to deal with kibble for right now. But I promise you, when we get home, it's a nice big juicy slab of beef for us. Okay?"

Li-Lou snorts and turns her back on me, her nose pointed toward the bathroom door. I put a couple of bottles of water and Motrin on a side table and set down another mug of steaming hot cocoa. Checking our clothes, I find they are dry—not that I want her to get dressed—but I supposed the offer should be there. I set a couple cans of soup down on the counter, make Li-Lou her kibble and grab the first aid kit before finally knocking on the bathroom door.

"Are you okay in there?"

"Yeah, just cleaning up."

"Getting ready for me?" Dammit, I can't stop.

Brandi swings open the door completely naked, holding the blanket up in front of her without actually shielding her body from my view. "I had to rip the top to get this off."

I suck in my breath, but otherwise keep my composure. "I think your clothes are dry. Do you want them?"

"I suppose that would be the proper thing to do."

Oh damn. Is that an invitation? Please god, be an invitation.

"I'm not big on being proper," I say carefully.

She blushes, but doesn't look away. "I get that feeling about you."

I should grab her clothes without being told to do so.

Instead, I lean my back against the wall and cross my arms over my chest, blatantly taking in the view. She's fucking gorgeous. Full, round breasts with tight, pluckable nipples. An hourglass figure with round hips made to be held on to. Her body is soft and shapely, like a goddess fully formed.

"What are you looking at?" Her face is devoid of emotion. She doesn't look happy, nor sad, nor mad or embarrassed. Maybe its uncertainty clouding her features and masking her emotions. It's like she's giving me a test and I have no idea if I'm passing.

Fuck it. I might as well go for it.

The worst that can happen is she knees me in the balls and tells me to stay away from her until we can get out of here in the morning.

"I'm looking at you. Or was that not the point of your dramatic exit? You opened the door fully nude, clutching the blanket to your sternum but not actually covering up any of the parts I want to feast on."

"Feast on?" She arches a manicured eyebrow.

A sly smirk tilts up the corner of my mouth. "I want to devour every beautiful inch of you."

"Where would you start?" Her voice has the slightest tremble in it, and I wonder if she's nervous or cold.

I can heat her up really quick.

"Well," I step forward and brace my hands on the door frame, so even though I'm hovering over her, I'm not actually touching her—although I'm sure she can feel the heat radiating off my chest. "First, I'll start right below your ear, nibbling my way along your neck and down your clavicle before swirling my tongue around your breast and latching onto your pert nipple."

I mimic exactly what I'm saying without actually touching her. My breath caresses her skin, leaving a trail of wet heat on the path I fully intend to take later.

"Oh." She quivers, her nipple puckering tighter.

"Then, after playing with your nipples, sucking and biting until you're helplessly grinding your pussy against me, I'll claim your lips and use my tongue to coax a couple moans out of you."

I drop to a knee in front of her, my hands still braced against the doorjamb. Glancing up at her, the view from down here is inspirational. I'll definitely use this vision for future fantasies. "While you're moaning into my mouth, I'll slip my hand between your legs and use my fingers to see how wet you are for me."

She worries her lip, her breathing erratic while staring down at me.

Fuck me, I haven't even touched her yet.

I smirk, thrilled by the reaction she's having to me. "Are you wet, Brandi? A juicy peach waiting to be eaten? I love succulent fruit—especially when the juices drip down my chin."

I take in a deep breath and let it out slowly, inhaling her scent and letting it mark my soul. "Tell me what you want, beautiful, and I'll give it to you."

"I want you to fuck me."

"Good girl," I all but growl, sliding my hands off the doorjamb and onto her thighs.

"Girl?" she giggles. "I'm old enough to be your mother."

"You're not." I stand up, pull her out of the bathroom and then swing her into my arms. Carrying her to the couch, I realize I need to get her out of her head and over our age gap if we're truly going to enjoy ourselves. My job is to make her come so hard, so many times, she forgets everything except how I make her feel.

I hold her tight against my chest and press my mouth to her neck. "While I have you underneath me, while my mouth is on you, you are a girl. Specifically, you're *my girl*. So. you're going to need to fucking deal with it."

Setting her gently on the cushion, I hand her the mug of hot cocoa and drape a blanket over her before returning to the kitchenette.

"Where are you going?"

I grab a bowl and head out the front door, scooping up snow. We don't have ice, ironically enough, but we have Ziplock bags and plenty of snow. "While I am going to fuck you, Brandi, I still need to wrap your knee and ice it. Drink your cocoa and water and lie back while I take care of *my girl*."

Her eyes sparkle every time I say *my girl*, so I'm going to keep saying it until she either expects it, or we leave this mountain and go our separate ways.

Kneeling in front of her, I nudge her legs apart with a tap of my finger and set the heel of her injured leg on a footstool, grabbing the ace bandages. I wrap her knee in a thin layer to protect her skin, lay the bag of snow down and use another two bandages to secure it in place. Brandi watches me intently, a small smile curling the ends of her lips, the mug of cocoa in her hand. She already drank half a bottle of water and took the Motrin I had laid out for her.

"How does that feel?" I ask as I take the mug from her hands.

"It feels good. Thank you."

"You don't have to thank me. It's my pleasure to take care of you." I flip the bottom half of the blanket covering her and slide my hands around her hips, gently pulling her ass to the edge of the cushion.

She sucks in her breath, her lips parting.

"Do you want me to stop?" Flexing my fingers against her ass cheeks, I will her to say no. I mean, if she wants me to stop, of course I will. I might have to go lie down dick first in the snow for a couple minutes, but I'll stop, nonetheless.

She shakes her head. "No."

"Good girl." I lower my mouth to her thigh, but keep my eyes on her, watching her watch me. She holds her breath as I push her legs farther apart and move my way up, pulling her to me by lifting her ass in my hands. I serve her up like a hot pie fresh from the oven, my mouth watering for a taste.

But I'm really turned on by the shock and awe on her face.

Falling into bed with someone isn't her style.

This impromptu encounter is outside her comfort zone.

And yet, I think she wants to be wild.

I'm definitely the right guy for the job.

"I'm going to taste you now, Brandi. Are you going to come for me?"

"If you do a good job," she quips, a sassy smirk on her beautiful face.

"Are you issuing me a challenge? I'm willing to take any direction you give me, beautiful. Tell me exactly how you like it." I flatten my tongue and slide along her slick lower lips, wrapping my hand around her upper thigh and peeling her open with my thumb. With every lick, I go deeper until I'm tonguing and sucking on her engorged clit, and she's writhing against my mouth.

"That's it," I growl. "Give it to me. Fuck my mouth and take your pleasure."

"Oh, Linc." She slides her fingers into my hair and fists a handful of strands as she breaks apart. "Oh god."

Fucking hell. Brandi is juicy—a squirter—who shoots her arousal down my throat as she comes apart in my hands, and it's fucking glorious. I drink down every drop of her sweetness, groaning as I wrap my forearms around her thighs and pull her tight against my mouth like a parched man desperate for a drink.

Fuck. She's like ambrosia. I could drink every day and stay drunk on the taste of her, forever happy.

"Ahhh!" She pushes my head away. "Softer, babe. Give me a minute to catch my breath."

I must have a feral look on my face—I certainly feel like an animal right now—because one look and she grins. "I don't think you need any instruction from me."

A drop of her dribbles off my chin and I wipe it away

with my paw. "You should have warned me you're a drug. I could easily get addicted to you."

"I'm not a drug." She giggles as I climb back up her body.

"You are to me." I kiss her softly at first, testing and teasing. She threads her fingers into my hair, pulling me down on top of her. We're awkwardly splayed right now, her leaning back in an uncomfortable position with one leg up on a footstool. There is a bedroom, but there's no fireplace in there.

Fuck it. I'll keep her warm. "Want to move this to the bedroom?"

She nods. "Yes."

I stand up—my cock jutting out in front of me without apology—and lean forward to pick her up.

Brandi's eyes travel down my body, her mouth dropping open. "Wait."

"What?"

She reaches forward and trails her hand over my erection tenting the thick gray cotton and hooks her fingers into the waistband. With a simple tug, she frees me, a small gasp escaping her lips.

Yeah, I'm bigger than the average guy. I'm not a horse, but gasp-worthy, for sure.

I smile down at her. "Are you offended?"

She wraps her fingers around my cock and shakes her head. "I'm hungry."

"Don't bite down, and I'll feed you all I have and more."

She repeats my words from earlier. "I'll do whatever you want. Just tell me exactly how you like it."

"I'm pretty sure I'm going to like anything and everything you do to me, beautiful." I cup the back of her head as she opens her mouth and takes me deep.

"Ah, fuck," I groan. Her mouth is exquisite. And with the way she is working me, I'm not going to last long.

VETERAN
K9
TEAM
REPORTING
FOR DUTY

Chapter Six
Brandi

Linc is wild and uninhibited compared to my past lovers. Every relationship I've had in the last twenty-three years has been carefully brokered over lunch, followed by happy hour, followed by a later scheduled date at their place—never mine. Although I never hid my friends-with-benefits relationships from Betty, I certainly didn't flaunt them either. If she met one of them at a social event, normally a work gathering, she either didn't know who they were, or never let on.

Of course, finding men interested in friends-with-benefits was easy when I worked at the hospital. Doctors and nurses are very busy and work crazy hours, so relationships are extra hard. But since I moved to the nursing home, my potential *friends* have dried up.

I wrap my fingers around Linc's thick cock, taking him as deep as I can before licking and teasingly biting the head.

He hisses, his fingers flexing against my scalp.

I glance up, expecting him to have his head back, and eyes shut—but nope. Past the drool-worthy inches of ripped muscles, Linc has his head down and eyes open, an almost painfully focused expression on his face as he watches me.

Damn, that's hot and makes me feel like an uber seductive sex kitten. While I'm sure he works hard for his amazing body, the gods also blessed this man in every other way. His cock, for instance, should be bronzed in a museum. His face... Lucifer himself would weep. And his cocky, flirty, yet endearing personality equals soaked panties.

How a woman hasn't locked him down is beyond me. I'm sure it's because he's not a one-woman kind of guy and he wants to be free to play the field.

Damn. I bet he doesn't have condoms on him and I doubt there are any here. How am I going to handle that?

"Mmmm. You need to slow down, beautiful, or I'm going to come down your luscious throat," Linc groans as he fists my hair.

I double down my efforts without speaking a word, taking him harder and faster, pumping my hand up and down his gorgeous shaft.

"Ah, fuck." He pants, his ass and thigh muscles clenching as he shoots his load in my mouth. It slips past my tongue and down my throat before I realize he's coming and I make quick work of cleaning him up.

With a fist full of my hair, he pulls me off of him and claims my lips in a punishing kiss, pushing me against the back of the couch. "Damn, woman."

"I could become addicted to you, too."

He takes my hand and pulls me to my feet so I'm standing face to chest with him. Then he lifts me up. "Wrap your leg around my waist. We'll deal with the ice pack in the bedroom."

His cock is still hard and pressing perfectly against my opening. It will take nothing for him to slip inside of me. I bite my lip, clamping down the words threatening to spill out of my mouth that will ruin this entire thing.

I know I should be safe.

I know I should be careful.

But I want him so bad.

He carries me into the bedroom, lying me gently on the bed and covering me with his body. His hand is in my hair while he props himself up on one elbow, his delectable lips trailing kisses down my neck and over my breast. As promised, he swirls his tongue around until he latches onto my nipple, teasing and tormenting with small bites. He lavishes attention on one side, then moves to the other, until I'm grinding my pussy against his thigh and begging him for more.

"I don't suppose you have condoms?" I can't stop the words from coming out of my mouth.

"Are you worried about STIs or pregnancy or both?" He doesn't stop, replacing his mouth with his thumb and forefinger as he looks up at me.

"Both?" Temperance and desire war in my gaze.

"I'm not nearly the manwhore you think I am. I haven't been with anyone in a few months and I'm tested quarterly. And I can't get you pregnant."

"You can't?"

"No. I had a vasectomy at nineteen. There's a genetic marker for heart defects in my family and I was pretty sure I didn't want kids, anyway. At least not kids that I pass my fucked-up genes to." He slides his hand down my belly and in between my legs, the tip of his middle finger finding my clit with ease. "I might have condoms in my wallet, but I might not and I seriously doubt there are any here. Do you want me to look?"

"A couple of months?"

He makes a show of thinking about it. "We broke up on September sixth and hadn't had sex for a couple of weeks before that. However, if you're having second thoughts, I'll gladly spend the evening eating your pussy and getting you off over and over again."

"No, I want you. Badly. But I was a teen mother and I'm still very fertile, so I'm extra careful."

"That's understandable."

I arch into his touch, my insides tightening as I get closer to the edge. "This isn't something I normally do."

"I can tell. But you can't deny the attraction between us, or your desire to let loose and be wild for once in your life." He flashes me a cocky grin. "Believe it or not, I don't fall into bed with random women either. I knew it when I saw you yesterday that I wanted you."

"I was wild once. That's how I ended up with Betty at seventeen."

"And I'm sure it was hard, but also well worth it."

I smile. "Absolutely."

He kisses me with reserved passion, exploring my mouth lazily, as if we have all the time in the world.

I suppose we do.

His kisses are intoxicating, his lips luscious, and tongue wicked. My body is primed to release again as he slips his finger from my clit and into my pussy, curling and stroking my inner walls. "Are you going to come for me again?"

"Yes." I moan softly and clutch his biceps.

"Not yet." He slides down my body, replacing his fingers with his mouth, latching onto my clit and taking my orgasm from gentle to mind-blowing in a matter of minutes.

Good god, this man has a magical tongue.

"Oh, Linc." He pushes my good leg up, always careful of my ice-packed knee and thrusts his tongue inside of me, my climax exploding and shattering me from the inside out.

Once again, I'm falling to pieces for this man, confident he'll pick me up and put me back together. Wow... I don't think I've had this kind of faith in a man since David, who broke my trust in all men.

"Fuck. I love the way you come."

"Mmmm. And I love how you make me come. I don't think I've ever been this wet before in my life."

"You don't squirt every time?" Linc places kisses against my belly while yanking blankets haphazardly over us. It is a tad cold in here without the fireplace.

"Squirt?" I scoff, almost offended and definitely embarrassed. "I don't squirt."

He chuckles. "Yeah, you do and it's the sexiest thing I've ever seen."

Oh? He likes it?

"I've been soaking wet a few times, but no one has ever said I..." Even saying the word sounds weird.

"Well, you've done it for me twice. I guess I'm special."

He has no idea. I rarely come from oral, so he's super special in my book. He lies beside me and kisses me while trailing his fingers over my breasts.

I reach down to find him painfully hard. "Don't you want to fuck me?"

"Do you want me to fuck you?"

"Yes."

"Even without a condom?"

I stroke my fingers down his stubbled cheek. He's so young and vibrant and confident—all the things I never was, not even at his age. "Yes."

"Good, because I know for a fact I don't have one in my wallet. And one wouldn't be enough with you, anyway."

"You were prepared to not have sex?" I love the fact we can talk even while I'm fisting his cock and he's plucking my nipples.

"I told you, I will go down on you every fifteen minutes until I get lockjaw or you run dry and be perfectly happy. Do I want to sink my cock deep inside you? That would be an emphatic yes. Can I control myself and go without if that's what you need and want? Begrudgingly, also yes."

"I trust you. And believe me, having my trust is a big deal." I grin, pressing the pad of my thumb over his swollen head and rubbing pre-cum into the ridge at the top.

"You can trust me to take care of you in all ways, Brandi." He shifts his weight and settles his hips between my legs. "This might be a little awkward with your knee."

"Actually, can you unwrap it? I'd like to be free to move it, if I can."

Arching his brow, he nods. "Okay, but don't let me hurt you."

Only my heart because this is the kind of man I could fall in love with. I have butterflies fluttering around in my tummy, similar to how I felt as a sixteen-year-old with her first boyfriend—her first everything.

"I won't let you hurt me," I say without conviction.

He unwraps my knee, tossing the bandage and melted pack of ice to the floor. I tentatively bend it. It hurts, but it's manageable and allows me to spread my legs wide for Linc.

Grinning, he slides his hands up my inner thighs, over my hips and then lays his palms flat on the mattress on either side of me. Holding his body over mine, he stares down. "You are really beautiful. I love your eyes and your skin and your plump lips."

Then Linc kisses me passionately, his tongue dancing with mine like two lovers who already know each other intimately. In this moment, I feel so comfortable with him that I melt into his touch, my mind and body lost in the exquisite love Linc has to give.

His cock prods against my opening and then hits just right, slipping inside without the awkward fumbling around. I gasp into Linc's mouth as he growls and jerks his hips, sliding deeper with each thrust.

"Ohhh." My voice shakes as he fills me and then some.

"Fuck, Brandi. You fit me perfectly." Linc's hazel eyes are on mine as he slowly withdraws and then pushes back in, harder and deeper each time.

"Perfectly," I murmur, half out of my mind with pleasure. Gasping with each stroke, I'm transfixed by the way he watches me, his eyes missing nothing.

He's not hurrying, not jack-rabbiting in and out of me like a man on a mission, but his movements are languorous, as if he is exploring fresh territory and cataloging the feel of every nerve ending.

"Definitely worthy of being addicted to. I might have to check into rehab after this." His voice is deeper, thick and smooth like peanut butter frosting.

I giggle and roll my eyes. "You're stupid."

He grins. "For you? Yeah. I am."

I close my eyes, his gaze too intense for my fragile heart, which up to this point I thought was solid rock. "Ohhh," I moan. "Good. You feel so good."

"Are you going to come for me one more time?"

Opening my eyes, I give him a sad shake of my head. Even though I feel out of my mind with pleasure, the reality is not likely. "I don't come from penetration."

He arches his brow. "Oh? Something for me to work for."

I snort. "I'm not trying to challenge you. Just being honest."

"I don't see it as a challenge, Brandi. I see it as a goal with the ultimate reward." He slides his hand between us and presses it flat over my pubic bone, his thumb pressing tight little circles against my clit. Between the slow, satisfying, consistent rubbing of the head of his cock against my G-spot and his thumb teasing my plump clit, I'm on the verge of orgasming for a third time in sixty minutes. Never in my life have I come so many times in such rapid succession and I wonder if being rung dry is an actual possibility.

"That's my girl. I feel you tightening up around my cock, desperate to explode for me."

"Are you close?" I moan, tossing my head back as he shifts his hips, hitting me a little different inside.

He shakes his head. "No, but having you come will definitely help me get there."

"Must be nice to have a young man's vigor."

"What did I say about fixating on our age difference?"

"I'm not fixating, but I'm impressed by your prowess."

Linc nuzzles my neck and nips at my earlobe. "You're lucky you messed up your knee, otherwise I'd put you over my thighs and spank your ass."

Something about the look on my face must give away more than I mean to because he smiles. "You like that idea, don't you? You like the idea of being put over my lap and spanked. What other little kinky desires do you have rolling around in that beautiful head of yours?"

Shaking my head, I say nothing, but he's not wrong. The idea of being handled by a man in bed has always turned me on, but I've never been bold enough to ask for it and none of the relationships I've had over the last twenty-something years have been the kind to explore the wilder side of sex.

But the look on Linc's face says he knows, and he will not drop the subject.

VETERAN
K9
TEAM
REPORTING
FOR DUTY

Chapter Seven
Linc

The look on Brandi's face tells me I want more than one night. I'll need weeks, maybe years, to unlock all her secrets and explore all her desires. The idea of tying her up, stretching her out, teasing and tormenting every inch of her—spanking, flogging, wrapping her in pretty ropes while I fuck her delectable mouth—goddamn every little detail takes me from hard to fucking coming in the matter of seconds.

She breaks apart first, bringing me to the edge. "Ohhh, Linc. Linc, no. I mean, yes. I mean, oh my god!"

I love the way she falls apart when she comes. A couple more thrusts of my hips and I'm joining her, gritting my teeth and burying my face in her neck as her cunt pulsates around me. "Fuck."

I'm holding both of her legs up with my forearms, her left knee held steady so I jostle it as little as possible, but her right knee is practically pinned to her ear and I have to say, I'm thankful she's flexible because I have a desire to bend her in all kinds of impossible positions tonight.

I collapse on top of her, panting for breath.

"Oh god. I don't think I've ever come so many times in a row in my whole life." she half moans, half sighs.

I smile against her neck and gently let her legs down, sliding to her right side. I roll her to me, cradling her left knee on my hip. "Good. But I'm not done with you yet, so I hope you're prepared to come a lot more before we get back out into the snow in the morning."

Using my fingertips, I brush her hair from her cheek and trace her jaw and lip, taking in her beauty. There's something about her that is special. I knew it yesterday when I saw her, but now, as I look into her beautiful face with its sated expression and dreamy eyes, I know this is more than insane lust. Looking at her is like looking at my future and I don't exactly know why.

She smiles, kissing my fingertip as I make another pass over her plump bottom lip. "I'll come as many times as you can make me."

"Challenge accepted."

She giggles. "I'm not challenging you."

"No. You're giving me goals."

We spend ten minutes relaxing and staring at each other, but the room is too cold to lounge around. "I'm going to drag this mattress into the living room so we have a nice bed to lie on in front of the fire. How does that sound?"

"It sounds like heaven."

"Great." I untangle us and jump out of bed, pulling

the blankets tight around her. "Give me a minute and I'll make the couch comfortable for you."

"You know, I'm not a complete invalid. It's just a twisted knee," she says as she pushes herself up into a seated position.

Placing my hands flat on the mattress, I lean forward and put my nose to hers. "I thought you liked me taking care of you."

She frowns, her eyes drifting off to the left for a second. "I said something like that, didn't I?"

"Amongst other things."

"What other things?"

I chuckle. "Well, I offered to make my muscles dance for you and you asked me what else I can make dance."

She bites her lip. "I think you showed me that dance."

"Oh, I have many moves left to show you." I press a kiss to her lips and then jog out of the bedroom, pushing the sofa back from the fireplace to make room for the love nest I'll make for us.

God, if any of the other guys that share this cabin saw what I was doing to it right now, they would kill me.

Oh well, it would be a glorious and well-earned death.

Once I have us settled on the mattress on the living room floor, the fire freshly stoked, I lie on my side with my head propped on my hand, looking down at Brandi with her golden hair fanned out over the pillow.

Li-Lou curls up on a pile of blankets above our heads, her ever watchful black-rimmed blue eyes on us.

"Tell me more about yourself." I slowly caress her body, unable to keep my hands to myself.

She runs her fingers through my hair, scraping her nails against the stubble on my cheek. "What do you want to know?"

"Were you ever married?"

"No. Betty's dad took off a couple of days after she was born."

I shake my head and mutter, "Fucking bastard."

She shrugs. "I think he wanted to be a good guy, but in the end, he couldn't do it. He wanted to be a man and in his head, he thought he could take on a family and make it work, but I think the reality of holding another human being—one he created—made him realize he couldn't do it on his own. Ultimately, he ran back to his family and six months later he got some other woman pregnant."

That's her first relationship? First love? A selfish asshole. That's too bad. She deserves so much better. "No other marriage proposals?"

"I haven't dated—not while Betty was living at home. I didn't want to risk a man coming into the house and changing the life she and I built together."

"So, just casual relationships over the years?"

"A girl has needs."

"I get that." I slip my hand between her legs again, lazily playing with her pussy—because I can.

"What about you? Have you made any grand gestures?"

"No. I've never come close. I dated a couple of

women for six to twelve months at a time, but we deployed a lot when I was in the Army, so those relationships never lasted long and I haven't met the right woman in Spring City."

"You will. Outside of being devastatingly handsome, you're a nice guy, too."

Maybe I already have? I think, but keep to myself.

"Where do you live when you're not stuck on top of mountains with devastatingly handsome men?"

She chuckles. "I live in Arizona."

"What brought you to this mountain out of all the ones you could've gone to?"

"Betty moved to Spring City a couple months ago, and I came to visit her for the holidays and my birthday."

"When's your birthday?"

She blushes. "Tuesday."

"Happy early birthday, beautiful." I lean down and give her a kiss.

Reaching under the blanket, she wraps her delicate fingers around my semi-hard cock which has yet to deflate in her presence.

"It certainly is happy."

"How long are you in Colorado?" I flex my hips and arch into her hand—fully erect in three quick strokes.

"Through the new year."

"You could get that much time off from the hospital?"

She frowns. "I might have overstated what I do for a living. I'm not an RN, but a CNA, and I no longer work at a hospital, but at a senior care nursing facility."

"Still, getting a month off of work isn't easy."

"Well, they knew they either needed to give me the time or I was quitting."

"Do you think you'll move to Colorado?"

"Are you asking me out on a date, Linc?"

"Maybe." I smile. "Definitely."

"The point of Betty moving away was to give us some space to have our own lives. I don't think she'd be very happy if I followed her here. But the next time you're in Arizona, look me up." She smiles and my heart breaks a little.

"I'll do that. I've always wanted to go to a stateside desert. While I've spent enough time in the sandbox overseas, I've never played in our sand."

"Well, Arizona doesn't have a lot of sand. It's mostly hard-packed dirt."

"Then I guess we'll stay in the air-conditioning under the covers."

"Sounds perfect to me."

I claim her mouth again, slipping my tongue past her lips. Rolling on top of her, I pull her legs up and slide inside, making love to her again.

I can't seem to do it any other way. I could blame it on her knee—a subconscious desire to protect her and ensure I don't inflict any pain—but there's more to it than that. The desire to go fast and get off is nonexistent with Brandi. I want to worship her, devour her, absorb her until she stains my spirit and permeates my soul. She's perfect for me, but she's only temporary, unless I can convince her to want more.

To want me, and possibly forever.

Her climax builds and I purposely keep my hands away from her clit, the head of my cock stroking against her spongy inner walls and swollen g-spot.

"You feel so good," she whines as her pussy clamps down. I continue to drag myself in and out of her, hitting her just right over and over to coax one orgasm and another out of her. For a woman who didn't believe she could come from penetration, much less have multiple orgasms, she just did both with me.

If that doesn't convince her we're perfect together, nothing well.

I stop and smile down at her while her cunt milks me for seed I no longer have to give. "And you said you couldn't come from penetration."

"Holy shit. That was..."

"The key is not overthinking it, beautiful. Not all orgasms are mind-blowing. Some of them are mild tiny explosions, like rapid fire. Rat-a-tat-tat-tat." I grin down at her when she giggles. "Now the question is—how many in a row can we get you to have?"

We wake up with the full sun shining through the windows. The fire burned down to golden embers a while ago. Without thinking, I slide my hand between her legs and wrap the arm she's sleeping on around her breasts, pulling her back against my chest. We made love all night, and I finally fell asleep dreading the morning sun.

"Good morning," she murmurs.

I kiss her neck, her shoulder and press my hardened cock against her ass.

She giggles drunkenly. "Again?"

"What can I say? You turn me on."

"What time is it?"

"Daytime," I say as I lift her thigh and slide into her from behind.

"Ohhh." she moans and arches her ass into me, allowing me to push deeper.

Unlike last night, this morning I feel hurried, frantic, clawing after something just out of my reach. I pump my hips fast and hard into her, circling her clit with my middle finger, pushing us toward our release. Brandi cries out at the same time as I groan, shooting cum deep inside of her. My arms band around her, pinning her to my chest and yet I pump my hips through my orgasm, continuing my savage assault on her.

And that's when I realize what I'm doing. I'm claiming her, marking her—a predatory need taking over as I clamp my teeth down on her bare shoulder.

She's mine—and I don't want to let her go.

"Ow!" Only her crying out in anything other than ecstasy clears my mind, reminding me where I am and who I'm with.

"Sorry, beautiful. I don't know what came over me."

Glancing over her shoulder, she looks at me with confused eyes. "Are you okay?"

"Yeah. You felt so fucking good. I lost control."

Li-Lou whimpers from her bed above our heads. I look up to find her judging me with her piercing blue eyes. Or maybe I'm projecting my guilt onto my dog. She has a very expressive fur face.

"Does she need to go out?"

Maybe, but that's not what the whimper and look are about. Right now, Li-Lou is calling me an asshole, and she's probably right.

"Probably. She's held it like a good girl for a long time." I roll over and grab my watch from the couch, glancing at the time.

"Fuck," I mutter.

"What time is it?"

"7:30. We're so late."

Begrudgingly, I let Brandi go, and extricate myself from the blanket, grabbing the radio along the way. One missed call from dispatch twenty-five minutes ago.

Damn, I'm surprised they haven't knocked the door down yet.

I grab the pair of sweatpants and pull them on, dialing up dispatch.

"Is that you, Linc?" Sherri, who was working shift yesterday around this time, chirps with her bright, youthful voice.

"Yeah. I just woke up."

"We've sent a party out for you and the desert dweller, Ms. Appleton."

"No need. We're good. I'll wake her up and we'll ride down after I dig the snowmobile out."

"Actually, they're already up there digging their way to you. Apparently, you have a six-foot drift piled against your front door."

I glance around the room at all the windows. Snow is piled up at least halfway. Shit, how did I not notice that? It wasn't like that when it stopped snowing last night, but the winds must've picked up after we fell asleep and whipped the fresh falling snow around into a frenzy.

"Who's outside right now?"

"Talbott and Holman," she replies.

Fuck!

Fuck, fuck, fuckety, fuck!

Holman hates me and will definitely report me if he gets a whiff of any wrongdoing on my part.

"Okay. Did they give you an ETA on how long it'll take for them to dig us out?"

"They didn't say. It could be twenty minutes. Could be two hours."

"Roger. Thanks." I throw the radio on the couch and crouch down next to Brandi.

"Hey beautiful, it's time to get dressed."

"Okay." Brandi tosses me a confused look, but I don't give her time to ask me a question. I pull the blankets off her and throw them at the couch. Helping her up, I hand over her clothes and tell her to get dressed in the bathroom while I put the cabin back together. I'm a flurry of activity as soon as she closes the door, hoisting the mattress up in the air and carrying it back to the bedroom. I move the couch back in place and then call Barron to give him a heads up.

God knows what he got into last night, but I'm betting if he had his way, it was a lot like my night.

"Barron? Do you read me?"

"Yeah, man."

"We're going to be out of here soon."

"Everything good?"

"Yeah, a team came to dig us out. I don't know how long it's going to take to get out of here, though."

"How much time do you think I have?"

"An hour. Maybe two."

"Roger. See you when you get here."

"Out."

Fuck. I wish I had some air freshener because something tells me this cabin smells like sex.

VETERAN
K9
TEAM
REPORTING
FOR DUTY

Chapter Eight
Brandi

Linc is a little frantic this morning, shoving clothes in my arms and hustling me into the bathroom. I swear it only takes me five minutes to clean up the best I can and get my clothes on, but when I come out of the bathroom, he's made the bed, pushed the couch back in place and is in the middle of folding blankets.

"What's going on?"

"There's a team outside digging us out. If they caught me lying naked with you, I'm pretty sure somebody would have my ass."

"Oh. Yeah. I can see how that might be a problem."

"Yeah, so..." He drops the blankets and walks over to me, pushing me backwards until we're both standing in the bathroom. He kicks the door shut, cups my face, and lays a fervent kiss on me. "I really wanted to lie in bed with you all day today."

"I really want to take a shower with you."

"That would've been nice."

"Maybe you and I can sneak into the house we're renting and take a shower in my bathroom? It's a really nice shower." I waggle my brows.

He wraps his arms around my waist and slides his hands down my ass, pulling me against him, the bulge in his pants obvious. "That's a fantastic idea."

There's a heavy knock on the front door.

"Shit." he hisses. "Stay in here for a couple minutes and then come out."

I nod. "Okay."

He closes the door and I check my face, using the washcloth to do a half ass job of brushing my teeth before pressing my ear to the door.

"Your chariot awaits, princess," a grumbly male voice barks.

"Holman, you romantic son of a bitch. I knew you liked me." I can envision the smirk playing on Linc's lips.

"It would be unethical of me to let somebody die on my mountain."

Oh... the newcomer does not sound happy.

"Your mountain?" Linc goads. "Isn't it our mountain?"

"Fuck you, Linc. Where's the desert dweller?"

"She's in the bathroom, but outside of a twisted knee, she's good to go." Linc's voice comes closer, so I assume they're both in the house now.

There's a pause. "You didn't cross any lines up here, did you?"

Linc's voice goes from light and jovial to sharp. "Oh, you'd love that. Wouldn't you?"

"I'd love to make you go away. I know you fucked at least two of those girls from Florida last year."

My jaw drops, and a small gasp escapes my lips.

He is a manwhore, after all. My heart breaks a little, which is stupid. I have no claim on Lincoln, despite how passionate and personal our night together felt.

Linc brings his voice down so low, I can't pick out his words. Swinging open the bathroom door, I make a show of hobbling more than necessary, locking eyes with the stranger and avoiding eye contact with the man who pleasured my body and broke my heart. "Our savior."

The new guy is closer to my age, maybe a little older, although it's hard to tell. The sun and harsh cold air—patches of red, chapped skin near his mouth and temple—weathered his face long ago. "Ma'am. Are you okay?"

"I'm great. I'm alive because of Lincoln and Li-Lou. If they hadn't found me when they did, I surely would've died yesterday."

"Do we need to take you to the hospital?" He approaches me, his eyes scanning my body from head to toe. I'd like to say he's assessing me with a clinical eye, but that's not the vibe I get from him—and it creeps me out.

"I'm fine. I'd like to go to my house so I can shower and put this entire experience behind me."

"We should wrap your knee again before we go driving down the mountain to protect it from jostling and the elevation drop." Linc steps forward, his eyes searching my face.

"If you think that's best." I hobble into the bedroom and sit on the edge of the mattress.

Linc follows me with the ace bandages he pulled off me last night.

"Can you do it over the pants and make it tight enough to provide me support down the mountain? I'm going to remove it as soon as I get into the house, anyway." I ask, aware the other guy is hanging around outside the door, listening.

"Sure." Linc's eyes searching mine. When I lock gazes with him, he mouths, "Sorry about that."

I shrug and put a placating smile on my face, but deep down, I'm experiencing my second bout of heartbreak in twenty-three years.

Dammit, how could I have let myself fall so quickly?

Stupid. Stupid. Stupid, Brandi.

Linc helps me into my boots and hands me my jacket, his demeanor completely different in front of the men who came to rescue us.

"Hey, man. How was the night?" A second man enters the door. He's covered in snow and is a lot closer to Linc's age than the other guy.

"It went fine. Someone stocked this cabin well at the end of the season."

"Yeah, it's part of the summer-to-winter shift we do." The man nods in my direction. "Ma'am."

Linc rubs his hand down his face. "Are we ready to go?"

Holman steps forward to address me. "Do you want to ride with me, ma'am?"

"No," Linc damn near growls. "I've got her. Talbott, can you take Li-Lou down with you to the lodge?"

"No problem," the younger guy responds.

Ten minutes later, they extinguished the fire and wood-burning stove and locked the cabin up tight. Linc has me settled in the sidecar of his snowmobile, a waterproof tarp covering me from the neck down with a weird hood strapped over my head. I'm unbelievably warm, considering the freezing temperatures outside.

Honestly, it's a beautiful day and the skiers are out in force, gobbling up the fresh powder. Under any other circumstances I'd be jealous, but I'm not sure I'll ever play in the snow again after this experience. Donning skis will only remind me of Linc, and I'm not sure that's a memory I want to hold on to.

We get down the mountain in record time, pulling into a snowmobile carport near the ski in/ski out backdoor of the house. Linc jumps out of his seat and unwraps me, lifting me in his arms and carrying me into the mudroom. "Are you okay?"

"Yes. Thank you." I'm trying to keep my voice light, but my heart is heavy.

"I'm so sorry about that. Holman hates me and is always looking for a reason to fuck with me." Linc kneels down and pulls off my boots. He never buckled them and carried me to and from the snowmobile, so they come off easily.

He pulls off his heavy winter boots and walks with me into the house where we're confronted with the image of my daughter riding a man in the hot tub.

"Oh my god!" I squeal, my voice pitching high.

The man wraps his arms tight around Betty, shielding her from our view.

Betty looks over his massive shoulder with big, wide eyes. "Mom?"

"I'm so sorry." I turn away to find that Linc already has his back to them.

The man's voice is a deep growl. "Linc?"

"Yeah." Linc chuckles next to me.

"You better have your back turned."

More chuckling. "It is."

They murmur to each other, the jets of the hot tub muffling their voices. "Mom, can you give us a few minutes?"

I'm completely flabbergasted and unsure of what I should do. I mean, Betty's an adult, but I certainly never expected to see her like this. "Yes, sweetheart. Of course. I'm so sorry."

"Wait. Why is your knee wrapped up?" Betty snaps.

I sigh, moving toward the stairs. "That's a story for when you and your friend are dressed. I'm going upstairs to take a shower."

Linc stuffs his hands in his pockets and shrugs, his eyes on me. "I guess I'll head back to the lodge and check in with dispatch. See you in a bit, Barron."

"I'll walk you out." I close the door to the mudroom behind me and bury my face in my hands. "Oh my god."

Linc chuckles. "Looks like everyone had a toasty night."

"Do you know that man?"

"Yeah, he's my partner. He's a good guy. You have

nothing to worry about with him." Linc pulls me into his arms and rests his chin on top of my head. We haven't spent a lot of time standing up and our height difference is noticeable now. "I guess we're not taking that shower."

"No." I shake my head, melting into his warmth. Part of me wants to push him away; part of me wants to cling tightly and never let go.

"Are you going to give me your phone number? Maybe we can go out a few times before you leave town."

"We're leaving on Tuesday."

"Yeah, but you're staying in Spring City until the beginning of the year, right?"

"Yeah."

"Brandi, I live in Spring City."

"Oh." I rattle off my phone number, positive he's never going to call. And even if he does, I'm not sure I should answer. The fact that he lives in Spring City and I didn't know that, while knowing exactly what his cock feels like giving me multiple orgasms is a problem in the morning light. I should at least know the basics like where he lives and what he does for a living when not rescuing desert dwellers from blinding snow storms.

"Wait." He lets go of me and pulls his phone out of his pocket. "Say it again."

I do, and he smiles before slipping his phone back into his pocket. "You have a text waiting from me."

"Okay." I press my lips together and wrap my arms around my midsection, effectively shutting myself off from him.

"Are you?" He cups my cheek. "What's wrong?"

"Nothing." I shake my head. "I think the adrenaline of the entire experience is finally wearing off and I really need to lie down."

Linc wraps his hands around my head, his thumb pressed under my chin, forcing me to tilt my face up to look at him. "Take a hot shower, ice and elevate your knee, and get some sleep, beautiful. Obviously, I'd prefer to tuck you in—"

"I'm a grown woman with an adult kid. On Tuesday, I'll be forty years old. I think I know how to take care of myself!" I snap and take a step back. "Sorry. I'm exhausted. Thank you for everything, Lincoln."

I turn and enter the house, closing the door behind me to leave him standing there to do whatever. I hustle up the stairs like the hunchback climbing the Notre Dame tower to ring the bell, shedding clothes as soon as I hit the landing.

In the privacy of my luxurious custom shower, I cry.

Dammit—I can't remember the last time I cried anything other than happy tears. Betty's high school and college graduation—happy tears. When she got a six-figure job offer in Colorado—happy mixed with sad tears. But this is reminiscent of the tears I shed for weeks after David left, only this time I know I'll be okay.

It hurts, but I'll be fine.

Linc didn't leave me with a baby to raise on my own —just a broken heart, one he's not even at fault for breaking. This is on me—all on me.

Finally, I turn off the water and wrap a towel around

myself, taking a seat on the edge of my bed. Betty knocks gently before walking in. "What happened?"

I roll my eyes. "I got lost and hit a snowdrift. My ski got stuck in the snow while my body twisted in a circle, and I guess I sprained my knee. It'll be fine over time, but right now it hurts like the dickens."

"Do we need to go to the hospital?"

I bring my eyes up to hers. "Are you really going to pretend like I did not just walk in on you riding a very broad man in the hot tub?"

She blushes. "I figured we'd get to that, eventually."

"Who is he?"

"His name is Barron Theroux, and he was my ski instructor yesterday. He stayed with me when you didn't come home, and he's also Linc's Search and Rescue partner. They live in Spring City and train police dogs and other canines."

At least now I know what Linc does for a living, only I didn't learn it from him.

How embarrassing.

I nod slowly, biting down the questions swirling around in my brain. I'm in no position to question her actions, considering I spent the last eighteen hours being thoroughly fucked by a man almost half my age.

Okay, maybe not half, but certainly ten to fifteen years my junior, because once again, I never asked him his age. I barely asked him anything at all, yet had no problem dropping my blanket and offering myself to him.

I should be embarrassed, right?

Betty sighs and plops down next to me. "Oh, Mom. I think I'm in love."

I continue to nod, my mind whirling with questions and confessions and secrets. "You've never been a quixotic girl, so if you think you're in love, there's a good chance you are."

"What?" Betty stares at me, slack jawed.

I shrug. "Who am I to say what love looks like, Betty? I thought I was in love with your dad when he whisked me away to Arizona, but I think that was the dream of getting away from my overzealous family. They say when love hits you, it's like a lightning bolt. Many people say when they met their person, they knew it within seconds of meeting them. Did you?"

She does this half-nod, half-shake roll of her head. "As soon as our eyes met, I knew I wanted him. There was something special and I couldn't stop myself from teasing and flirting with him. He was completely on board, teasing me back."

"Well, if he also lives in Spring City, why not pursue something? Honestly, sweetheart, what do you have to lose at this point?"

Betty flashes me a smile that warms my heart. My baby girl is in love. "Tell me about your night."

I let out a weary sigh and shake my head. "That's another story for another time. I'm exhausted. I didn't get very good sleep last night, so I think I'm going to take eight hundred milligrams of ibuprofen, elevate my leg, wrap my knee in ice, and go to sleep."

"Would you like some hot tea?"

"That would be lovely."

"Okay. You get yourself situated and I'll grab you an ice pack and a hot tea."

"Thank you, my daughter."

"You're welcome, my mother."

As soon as she closes the door behind her, I change into flannel pajamas—the ones Betty bought me specifically for this trip—and climb into bed. I take the ibuprofen, elevate my knee, and thank my girl for the hot tea, waiting until she closes my door to pull out my phone.

Linc: I miss you already.

That's the text he sent from the mudroom.
Ten minutes ago:

I know something's wrong and I'm pretty sure I know what it is. Don't dismiss the connection we shared in the cabin. This wasn't just a one-night stand for me, so please don't ghost me, Brandi. I'm anxiously awaiting your return text, but if I don't hear from you before it's time for me to leave the mountain this afternoon, I will come find you. Don't make me carry you out of that bed and claim my shower with your daughter as a witness... because I will.

I consider not responding, but I also know Linc is a man of his word.

> Showered, warm and snuggled in bed with my knee elevated and ibuprofen pumping through my veins. I'm minutes from falling asleep and hope to sleep until dinnertime. Thank you for everything, Linc. Be careful driving down the mountain.

His reply is instant.

> This conversation isn't over, beautiful, but for now, I'll let you sleep. Dream of me and I'll talk to you soon.

He's being stubborn, but why?

Pulling away makes this super easy on him.

Why play with my heart?

The things I could say to him dance through my head. Snippets of conversations I've had over the years when my friends-with-benefits became too serious. Linc is no different from those men—besides infinitely better in bed—so one of my many excuses is bound to work on him. Given our age difference, geographic separation, and lack of having anything in common, entertaining more time with him makes no sense.

Time to harden my heart.

It should be easy.

So why does it feel impossible?

VETERAN
K9
TEAM
REPORTING
FOR DUTY

Chapter Nine
Linc

Fucking Holman and his big ass mouth.

The motherfucker has hated me since we met last February. Although he's been working Search and Rescue for Silver Mountain for nearly twenty years—way longer than Schmidt or Barron—he's pissed he's not in charge, and that our camaraderie got me the job he believes should have been his to give to his creepy, alcoholic buddy.

The women from Florida? Yeah, they clung to me, but not because they wanted me to fuck them. It was to get away from him. He was being pervy and flirting as if he had a chance in hell with any of the coeds from Florida State University.

Yes, they invited me back to their condo. Actually, they begged me to walk them home—which I did. I hung out for twenty minutes, did a couple shots with them and then walked back to my dorm and crashed in the bunk next to Barron.

I wasn't lying when I told Brandi I'm not a manwhore. Yes, I get plenty of opportunities. I'm a huge flirt—and let's face it, I look good—which makes tired, weathered old men like Holman green with envy.

Fuck him for making her question my feelings for her.

I get her reply text, the bands on my chest loosening the tiniest bit. She's trying to blow me off, but I will not have it. I'm a stubborn SOB when I want something and I want her.

I'm sitting in the truck with Li-Lou and Sarge while Barron stands in the lodge's alcove with his arms wrapped lovingly around Betty. I've never seen him with someone —not even his ex-wife. And although I've seen him talk to and even hook up a couple times at the bars over the years, I've never seen him hold on to someone like they are the air he breathes.

Shit. I guess I'm not the only one who fell hard this weekend.

We drive down the mountain in relative silence.

I know him. He won't talk to me about her and I'm in no position to tell him about what happened with Brandi. At least, not until I know where I stand with her.

He drops me and Li-Lou off at my car parked at the VKC, saluting me as he drives away. We get home twenty minutes later, but I wait until I'm settled for the night— laundry done, house cleaned, a juicy slab of beef in Li-Lou's and my belly—before texting Brandi.

Are you awake?

We both have iPhones, so I see when my message is read. She waits a couple minutes, three telltale bubbles alerting me she's writing a response.

After a couple minutes, she responds with:

I am.

No shit. I wonder how many replies she deleted before settling on that gem.

Are you alone?

Betty just went to bed.

I immediately dial her number, and she answers on the first ring.

"Hey, beautiful."

"Lincoln."

Dammit. How'd I get relegated back to a non-nick-name non-friend status?

I clench my hand into a fist. "Let's cut through the bullshit, Brandi. You're mad, or at the very least, hurt."

"I'm fine." Her voice pitches at the end.

"Lie." I tighten my jaw, visions of punching Holman in the face dancing through my head. "Talk to me. You think I lied to you about being a manwhore, but I didn't, and even if I had been one in the past, it doesn't change how I feel about you today."

"It's fine, Lincoln. We shared an amazing night together—one that wouldn't have happened in any other situation."

"Are you telling me that if I'd asked you out, you would've said no?"

She sighs. "Honestly, yes. I'm here with my daughter on vacation, and you are way too young for me any—"

"God dammit, Brandi. What did I tell you about letting our age difference affect your feelings for me?"

"I believe you said you would spank me."

"Don't tempt me, woman. I'll drive back up the mountain right now, yank you out of bed, and throw you over my knee."

She's silent for several seconds before she sighs again. "Why are you calling me? What do you want?"

"I want you," I blurt without thinking.

"That's impossible."

"No, it's not. Arizona is one state away. It's a twelve-hour drive or a two-hour plane ride."

"What are you saying?"

Sliding my hand down my face, I try to wipe away my frustration and get control of my feelings before I say something stupid or worse, hurtful. "I'm saying I want to take you on a date. I want to walk through a restaurant with you on my arm while motherfuckers stare and think *how'd that lucky bastard get someone like her?* I want to take you back to my place and make love to you all night long. And then I want to wake you with breakfast in bed, feeding you pancakes while I lick syrup from your pussy."

She gasps. "Oh god."

"And when your knee is better, I want to give you the spanking I think you're desperate to receive. I want to tie you up, bend you over, and fuck you hard—and afterwards, carry you into my hot tub and make love while staring into your eyes."

She snorts. "I don't think I'll ever look at a hot tub the same way again."

I laugh, the tension cut significantly with her little joke. "Fair enough. I'll have you ride my cock in my shower. The bench seat is the perfect height for us."

Brandi is silent again.

So silent, I have to check my screen to make sure she hasn't hung up on me.

Shaking my head, I grumble, "I didn't fuck Florida coeds last winter. Holman is a creep, and they asked me to stay close to keep him away."

"I got a creepy vibe off him," she whispers.

"Yeah? I'll take it out of his ass the next time I'm at Silver Mountain."

"You don't have to do that for me. I believe you, Linc."

Thank god we're back to Linc. I exhale a sigh of relief. "I know this is fast, Brandi, but I don't want this morning to be the last time I see you."

She lets out a shaky breath. "We know nothing about each other. I don't even know how old you are."

A low growl rumbles in my chest and I wish we were face to face for this conversation because I know she's going to make an issue out of our age difference, especially when there are actual numbers on the table. "I'm twenty-seven, and before you throw that number in my face as the reason we can't explore each other, I'm going to tell you that you're full of shit. Guys your age date women my age and younger all the time and no one bats an eye. And I'm not some pampered twenty-seven-year-old living in his mother's basement with no life experience. I'm betting there are fifty-year-olds out there that have gone through half of the shit that I have on and off the battlefield. I purposefully avoided bringing up my age because I didn't want it to be an issue, but understand me right now, Brandi, I will not let you push me away because of our age difference."

I'm met again with silence. "Did you practice that speech on your drive down the mountain?"

"Yes, I did, beautiful. What else do you want to know?" I put my phone on speaker and lean back against my headboard with my legs crossed at my ankles, my eyes shut as I send up a silent prayer that she gives us a shot—because I want nothing more right now than a chance at a relationship with her.

"I don't know," she says softly. "Yesterday you saved my life and then gave me more orgasms than I knew my body could have, but then this morning I realized I knew nothing about you. Maybe you should start with the basics."

"Like what?"

"Like—where are you from?"

Ugh. Talking about my childhood is not something I want to do over the phone. "I was born in Fort Smith, Arkansas."

"So, that is home?"

"No. It's where I was born and where I grew up, but

that's it. I guess Colorado is home until my *heart* takes me somewhere else." I emphasize the word because she needs to understand that I'm willing to go anywhere if and when necessary. Obviously, I would prefer to stay in Colorado with my Army brethren, but for the right woman I could easily become a desert dweller. "Where are you from?"

"I was born in Brigham City, Utah, but I've lived in Phoenix longer."

"Do you miss Utah?" I ask, the conversation flows the more we relax.

"No. I'll never go back there." She pauses, as if she's said too much, but then continues. "My family disowned me when I got pregnant with Betty, and they've never once checked on me or her. So... fuck them."

"That's how I feel about Fort Smith." I let out a slow breath and reveal some of my truth. "In the eight years I've been gone, I've gone back twice to see my mom. I suppose if she calls and asks, I'll go, but I'm not holding my breath. She and I didn't have the healthiest of relationships in my teenage years, and my dad never claimed us considering his other family—the ones he stepped out on with my mom—hated our very existence."

It's weird. My fucked up relationship with my mom isn't something I talk about, yet saying the words out loud to Brandi feels cathartic.

"I'm so sorry it's like that with your mother and father. I couldn't imagine my daughter not also being my best friend. We tell each other everything."

"Everything?" I tease.

"Well, maybe not everything. Although, if she asks me directly, I won't lie."

Are you going to tell her about us is on the tip of my tongue, but there's really no point if she refuses to see me again. "Let me take you out Tuesday night."

"Tuesday is my birthday."

"I know. I'm positive Barron will jump at the chance to spend the night with Betty. Celebrate your birthday with me and let me show you how good it can be between us when we're not snowed in at some Ranger Station cabin."

"Okay."

"Yeah?" I grin.

"Yes." I can't see her, but I know there's a smile playing upon her lips.

"Good. Now I can sleep knowing I'll have you in my arms again soon."

"You're crazy, you know that?"

Crazy in love... The words dance on my tongue, but I swallow them down. I can't freak her out and risk her running for the hills—or the cacti, as the case may be. "I'll text you tomorrow and see you on Tuesday, beautiful."

"Sleep good, Linc."

"Dream of me." I toss my phone on the bed and groan out loud.

Li-Lou lifts her head and smacks her lips, her blue eyes on me. Then she thumps her paw on my thigh. I run my fingers through her coat, scratching gently behind her ears. "This woman is going to be the death of me. She's perfect and I want her like I've never wanted a woman before. Is this love?"

Arrorrorrrooo. Li-Lou lies her head down on my thigh, speaking her piece.

When I was a teenager, I thought I was in love—or at least I said the words—but now, I'm not so sure I've ever felt anything close to it before. I know I've never felt struck like this before—as if my heart will shatter if I don't have Brandi in my life.

I know for a fact I'll do anything to make her mine.

Would she want me to move to Arizona? Who knows?

Would I do it? I'm thinking, yes.

Monday morning, I pull into the VKC parking lot right behind Barron. We walk side by side into the office to find Karden, Kemp, Vale, and Janey sitting around a large conference table with a huge aerial map of the property laid out in front of them.

"How'd the fundraiser go?" I ask anyone willing to answer. This last weekend, the VKC hosted a vendor fair and fundraiser, but Janey cut Barron and I some slack since we've been on the schedule at Silver Mountain since last March.

"We made twenty grand to go toward the PTSD training program." Vale looks up, throwing both of us a small head nod. "How'd your ski patrol weekend go? Heard you had a heavy snowstorm hit the slopes on Saturday."

Barron's eyes slide my way and a half smile parts his lips. We haven't shared one detail about our weekend, and he asked me no questions about Brandi, but then again, I wasn't the one caught with my pants down. "Linc had to rescue someone who got turned around in the whiteout conditions and got snowed in on the backside of the mountain overnight. Our young hero saved this woman's life."

"Good job, man." Kemp leans back and folds his massive biceps over his chest, tossing me an approving nod of his head.

My body heats with memories of "saving" Brandi, and my brain disconnects—stopping me from thinking through the ramifications as I blurt, "Barron had to save a hot chick from drowning in a hot tub."

"What?" Karden looks from me to Barron and back to me.

"You son of a bitch." Barron narrows his eyes and I swear if I was within reach, he'd pummel me.

"Come on, man. We gotta tell them." I grin sheepishly, hoping to charm my way out of trouble like I did when I was a kid. "It's too damn funny."

"What are you talking about?" Janey jumps in. She's been around guy-talk her whole life, and occasionally can be filthier than all of us combined.

"I walked in on him and his woman in a hot tub—" I punch my fist into my palm to demonstrate my point.

Barron's cheek flush red under his brown and silver speckled beard.

"No shit?" Kemp swings wide eyes up at Barron. "I didn't know you had it in you, old man."

"Fuck you," Barron says to everyone even though his gaze never leaves me.

Yeah, it doesn't matter if Brandi will start a relationship with me or not, because I apparently just signed my death warrant.

"I guess you don't want to talk about it?" Vale jokes.

"Nope," Barron grumbles as he walks over the coffeepot and fills his mug to the brim with dark brewed bitterness.

Yeah, I'm going to pay for this for a while.

Without speaking a word, Karden pushes a chair back from the table for me to sit down in . He's only a few months older than me and we came through AIT at the same time, but he is fully aware of how much trouble I used to get into.

"Dumbass." He chuckles under his breath and then bumps my fist under the table.

"What are we looking at?" Barron barks, looking down at the map purposefully.

They drop the hot tub conversation for the time being, but there is no way we won't be talking about it later when Barron is out training one of his clients. I can tell by the side eye going on around the table.

"This is the map of the property and the updated proposed changes after meeting with Logan on Friday."

Janey points to red circles drawn on a translucent overlay sheet.

"Did he finally admit he's rich?" I glance at Karden who knows Logan better than I do. He's the one who kept in touch with Hollywood and told him about the VKC—him or Saint, or maybe both. I know they deployed with him at the beginning of the year when they lost one of their guys while on patrol.

Actually, if I remember the story correctly, Logan was there with Saint when it happened.

"He didn't say where the money was coming from, only that he'd have it with him in January when he separated from the military and moved here," Kemp says.

"Shit. This is really happening. We're expanding." I separated from the military and moved here for barely minimum wage with the promise that when we expanded, we'd all get shares in the company—sometime within the next three years.

It hasn't even been a year yet.

"If we can secure the investors and buy the adjoining properties by late-January, we can start construction in May. One benefit of being outside city limits is we don't have as many zoning and construction permits to deal with." Janey and Kemp exchange a look that is above my pay grade, but I guess that's all about to change.

I wonder if Brandi would move here if I had a stake in a growing business. Once we do well at the center, I'd buy us a house and she wouldn't even have to work if she didn't want to, and...

I shake the runaway thoughts out of my head and pinch the bridge of my nose.

Slow the fuck down, Lincoln.

First, get her to agree to a couple dates, and then you can ask her to move in with you.

I've never been so sure about a woman in my life, but I know I need to be confident, yet patient with her, because I know if a woman came onto me like this, I'd back off quickly.

Later that evening, I drive past Barron's truck outside of Betty's apartment complex. I hop out and climb the stairs, knocking on #223's door with a bouquet in my hand and wondering how this is going to go down. Will Brandi greet me in front of her daughter with more than a friendly smile and a handshake? Will she try to play it off like we don't know each other intimately? Can I deal with it if she does?

Brandi opens the door, and I lean in and kiss her neck before she can sell this as casual.

This is not fucking casual.

"Hey, beautiful. Happy birthday."

"Oh... plot twist." Betty looks up at Barron with wide eyes.

Barron says something, but I don't catch what he says.

Brandi apparently does. "We do share everything, but I wasn't sure I'd hear from Linc again, so I saw no reason to tell her about our—"

"Need to keep warm," I say with a big smile, extending my hand to Barron.

He frowns and slaps my palm, but says nothing.

"Hey Betty." I offer her my hand.

"Hi again, Linc."

"I hope you don't mind, but I really want to take Brandi out for her birthday."

Betty shakes her head and squeaks, "No, it's fine. Where are you going?"

"Dinner and live music." I glance at Brandi and she nods. "I would've suggested dancing, but that's not possible given the circumstances."

"No, not today."

"Maybe next time."

The four of us stand in awkward silence when Barron grabs a wine glass and hands it to me. "I assume this is for him?"

"Oh, yes. Thank you," Brandi says.

I lift the glass. "A birthday toast?"

"Give it a crack, man." Barron motions for me to continue with a wave of his hand.

"To new beginnings and good times ahead of us." I lock eyes with Brandi, hoping to convey all I'm feeling and more with these simple words. "I hope this birthday brings everything you not only need, but deserve. Happy birthday, Brandi."

We take a drink and then I slide my hand onto the small of her back, letting it be known to all that she is mine. "We should get going."

"Okay. Let me put these in water and I'll be right out." Brandi takes her flowers and then hands Betty a bouquet that's sitting on the table. Both women scurry into the kitchen, leaving us alone.

Barron and I exchange a look. He shakes his head and hisses. "You son of a bitch. Talking shit at work for two days about me and you didn't think to mention your love life?"

I chuckle. "Hey, if you had caught me in a jacuzzi getting ridden by a hot chick, then I would've expected you to talk about it at work." I lower my voice and step closer. "As it is, we had planned to sneak into the house and shower together, but finding you two blew that bright idea all to hell."

Barron nods. "Okay, I guess we're even. Stop fucking talking about it at work and never call Betty a hot chick again."

"Roger." I toss back the last of my wine and put the glass down on the table. "By the way, I don't plan on bringing Brandi back here tonight."

"No shit." He throws me a look.

"And I'll call before I bring her home in the morning." I smirk. "To give you time to—"

"Stupid ass," he mutters.

I chuckle. "I see we brought the same flowers."

"Yeah, that's embarrassing."

"Well, at least they know what they're getting with us."

"Are we ready to go?" Brandi grabs her wallet and sets a giant bouquet—both of our flowers combined—down on the table in a pretty purple vase.

"After you, beautiful." I motion to the door, only then seeing Sarge.

Quickly, I bend down and scratch her ears. "Keep these two out of trouble, you hear?"

Sarge leans into my hand and gives it a lick before I'm out the door.

We're down the stairs and I'm helping Brandi climb into my car when she giggles. "What's so funny?"

"That was supremely awkward."

"I didn't think it was so bad."

"You didn't?"

"No. Although, if you'd told Betty about me before I came to pick you up, maybe that would've made things a little easier for you."

"I didn't know what to tell her. Honestly, I still don't."

"Don't you think your daughter wants what's best for you?"

"Of course."

"And don't you think I could be what's best for you?" I hold her gaze, reading into every little thought crossing her face. She's got twenty-plus years of doubt to wade through in order to accept me as the love of her life.

I already know she's the love of mine.

"Are you?" She licks her lips. "What's best for me?"

"I think so, and I aim to prove it to you. All you have to do is to be open to the idea of us and I'll do the rest."

"Okay."

I flash a grin and nod my head. "Okay. Put your seat-belt on."

I close the door, scoot around the hood, and slide into the driver's seat, but instead of starting my car, I lean over the center console and slide my hand into her hair, claiming her lips like I wanted to at her front door. Brandi melts into me like she did every time I touched her in our little mountain chalet, and although I know she's going to throw up the occasional roadblock, she's mine and no one is going to stop us from being together.

"Maybe we should skip dinner?" she says breathlessly.

"Oh no, baby. I'm taking you out and showing you off. I don't think you understand how absolutely stunning you are. You've gone too long without having a man adore you and I want to be that man."

VETERAN
K9
TEAM
REPORTING
FOR DUTY

Chapter Ten
Brandi

Linc says all the things I've only read in books or seen in sappy romance movies—and I love hearing every word. We go to a steakhouse that, if it's not the nicest in Spring City, it's in the top three. I am wearing a black knit sweater and a long, printed skirt that has a high slit on the side with black mid-calf boots.

He finds the slit after we're seated and slides his hand under my skirt and between my thighs. "I like this outfit."

I press my legs together, stopping the upward climb of his fingers. "Are you going to behave yourself in this fine establishment?"

I waggle my eyebrows, one hundred percent challenging him.

He shakes his head. "Not even a little."

Linc stationed me in the middle of the booth when we were seated by the hostess, and unless someone drops a fork and crawls under the tablecloth, they can't possibly see what's going on beneath the table.

"How does your knee feel? I noticed you were hobbling a bit, but it seems better than it was on Sunday."

"My knee feels pretty good. It hurts a little, but nothing I can't work through."

"Good. I'm glad there will be no lasting damage." Linc keeps his hand between my thighs as the server comes to take our order, flexing his fingertips and willing me to part my legs a fraction of an inch every couple seconds.

We place our orders, and he requests a bottle of wine. Once the server leaves, Linc turns toward me, pivoting on his hip in the seat. He slides his other hand over my thigh and push-pulls my legs apart, his eyes on mine. "You have no idea how badly I want to slip under this table and suck on your clit as an appetizer."

His words, coupled with the memory of his talented tongue, send a flood of warmth into my panties.

He grins, knowledge painting his face. "You're wet right now, aren't you?"

"Yes."

"Fuck." He slides his right hand between my legs, his fingers slipping behind the lacy scrap of fabric soaking up my arousal. He sucks in a ragged breath, using his other hand to grab mine and put it on his impressive bulge.

Desperation claws at me as I contemplate unzipping his slacks and pulling out his cock right now. I knead him through his trousers as he slips his fingers between my slick pussy lips to circle my clit.

"Ahhh," I moan softly.

He chuckles and casually looks around the restaurant. "Shhh, Brandi. You're going to get us kicked out of here."

As if I had my mouth full—and trust me, I want to—the server chooses this moment to return to the table with the bottle of wine.

Linc handles it perfectly, making eye contact and engaging the server while I bite down on my lip. If anything, I think he's circling my clit faster, rocketing me toward the edge.

He samples the wine and nods his head. "This will be fine. Do you want a sip, baby?"

I shake my head, not trusting myself to open my mouth. Clutching his thigh under the table, I break apart as soon as the server turns their back.

"Oh, fuck," I hiss through gritted teeth.

Linc slides his free hand into my hair and kisses me hard, swallowing my whimpers as I come on his fingers. "That's my girl. I fucking missed you."

Resting my forehead against his, I pant as he brings his hand up and sucks his fingers clean in front of the whole restaurant. If anyone is watching, they have to know what we're doing, and he doesn't seem to give one good goddamn what they think.

He grabs the wine bottle and pours us both a glass, handing one to me. "Happy birthday, beautiful. The first of many celebrations to come."

I'm not sure what he means, but I take a drink anyway. I'm not much of a wine connoisseur, so I'm pleasantly surprised I like the flavor of what he ordered.

"You know you're coming home with me tonight. Right?"

I grin behind my wine glass. "I figured as much, but I thought it would be a little obvious if I left the house with an overnight bag."

"I'll give you a change of clothes for tomorrow and I have everything else you need."

"Even my toothbrush?"

"I already bought you a new one specifically for when you stay at my place."

"Oh? You're planning on this happening more than once?"

"I have full expectations you'll not only stay with me every night you're here, but by the time New Year's Eve rolls around, I'll have convinced you to move here —permanently."

My mouth hangs open as the server comes back with our salads and a basket of freshly baked bread. Linc hooks his finger underneath my chin and pushes my mouth close.

I wait until the server leaves before shaking my head. "That's a lot of expectations, Lincoln."

"Are we back to Lincoln? I thought you were comfortable calling me Linc?"

"I am, but... you just ask you to move in with you."

"Yeah, I did."

"How can you be so casual about that? How can you be sure about me or us?"

Linc shakes his head and grabs both of my hands, pulling them into his lap. "There are no guarantees in life, Brandi. I learned that quickly in the military. We aren't guaranteed tomorrow, much less twenty years from now. What I know is how I feel about you today. You make me want things I've never wanted before. I want you. And I want forever with you."

"How are the salads?" The server comes up, but Linc doesn't take his eyes off of me.

"They're fine," he says.

Clearly, we haven't touched our salads, and thankfully, the server gets the hint and leaves.

"You want to slow things down and take this day by day—fine. You want to do the long-distance relationship thing?" He rolls his eyes. "I can work with it, but I won't like it. But if you think for a second, I'm going to let this be a casual fling, or a friend with benefits kind of sitch, you are very confused about the kind of man I am."

I'm rendered speechless by his monologue. Have I been treating him like a friend with benefits? I didn't think so, but I suppose subconsciously I have a clock hanging over our heads. I figured this would fizzle out by Christmas and we'd be over each other by New Year. Yes, I'd go home broken-hearted but sexually sated with a lifetime of memories to keep me warm while I figured out what was next.

He doesn't want fizzle. He wants heat and passion every day—with me.

"What, beautiful?" He cups my face and strokes my cheek with his thumb. "What are you thinking?"

"I don't know how to be in a relationship," I whisper, surprised by my own words.

"I know." He leans forward and kisses me softly. "Neither do I. Not really. But we'll learn together."

Linc grabs my wine glass and hands it to me. "Eat, drink, tell me stories about your life, and let's enjoy your birthday."

I take the glass and turn toward my salad, shaking my head. "Did I tell you I think you're crazy?"

He chuckles and slides one hand back on my thigh. "You might have mentioned it."

I've spent my life holding myself back from love and genuine connection because of one man who broke my heart before I was even legally an adult. I'm now alone—my home is an empty nest. If I don't dive headfirst into all Linc openly offers me—even if I think it's batshit crazy—then how will I ever kick start my life?

Taking a deep drink off my wine glass, I set it down and lean into him, kissing his neck right below his ear. "You are the craziest, sexiest, most confident, and domineering man I've ever met, Lincoln Abrams. And while I won't agree to moving in with you today, I promise I won't treat you like a casual fling. I'm open to falling in love with you and all that entails."

Linc kisses me hard with passion and adoration before softening his lips and sliding his tongue into my mouth. We kiss for longer than is publicly appropriate, but considering he got me off under the table and then licked his fingers for all to see, fuck what everyone thinks about our kiss. "That's all I'm asking for, Brandi."

We finish dinner without incident, but I convince him to skip live music by unzipping his pants in the car and crawling over the center console to wrap my lips around his thick cock. Now we're parked in a space sandwiched between two one-car garages with Linc's fingers in my pussy as I lick, suck, and pump him into my mouth.

"Fuck me, woman." Linc fists my hair and pulls me off of him. "Let's get inside."

He tucks himself into his pants and exits the car, opening my door before I can pull my skirt down. Next thing I know, I'm in his arms, being carried into his condo and set on my feet in a beautiful kitchen with custom cabinets and granite countertops.

"Hold on to the counter, beautiful, and spread your feet shoulder width apart." I do what he says, yelping when he yanks my skirt up to my waist and his tongue slides from the front to the back of my pussy before plunging deep inside me. He thrusts two fingers in, pumping so fast that I'm on the edge of coming within seconds.

"Not yet." He pulls his fingers free and replaces them with his cock, filling me hard and fast, his hands gripping my hips as he unleashes his inner beast on me. This reminds me of the last time we had sex, right after we woke up in the cabin. He was raw and animalistic, as if he was marking and claiming me.

I suppose that was exactly what he was and is once again doing.

"I want you coming on my cock."

"I'm close," I moan, bracing myself against the counter.

He fists a handful of my hair and pulls me back against his chest, one arm tight against my hips. "I fucking love you, Brandi. I know you're scared, but you are mine, and I'm never letting you go."

Something within me breaks apart and tears stream down my cheeks as my climax spills over the edge. "I love you, too." I cry out with my release, unable to hold back the emotions tumbling out of me.

Linc growls and clamps his teeth down on my shoulder again, pumping his hips as he shoots cum deep inside of me. He lets go of my hair and bands his muscled forearm around my chest, his bite turning into gentle kisses up my neck.

We pant in unison to catch our breath, words spoken aloud that can't be unsaid or unheard hanging in the surrounding air. He pulls out of me and turns me around to face him, his eyes a sparkling hazel. "I meant what I said. I love you."

My heart swells as I realize this simple truth. "I meant it, too."

He lets out a deep breath and smiles, interlacing his fingers with mine. "Let's go make love, beautiful. I'll feed you your birthday cake later."

VETERAN
K9
TEAM
REPORTING
FOR DUTY

Epilogue
Linc - Four months later

I walk through the security gate into the waiting area of the Sky Harbor airport. Brandi and I spent the end of November and all of December in each other's arms, and as far as I was concerned, life was perfect. I thought I'd convinced her to move in with me before she boarded the plane leaving DIA on January 2nd, but after only spending one weekend together in the last six weeks, she now wants to wait.

The long distance thing has been utter fucking torture, and the time apart has caused her to reflect on our relationship as more of a fantasy and not the future I'm envisioning. Too much distance has given Brandi time to question our compatibility and love.

I know she loves me.

She says she believes I love her.

But she also wants to live and date in the same city before we move in together and take that next step.

We will wait, because what other choice do I have

but to be patient and shower her with all the love and affection I can—every chance I get?

At least she's moving to Spring City this week, so we can jump forward into the next phase of our forever. I flew down here to pack her up and drive her home—not to my place, like I hoped, but to Betty's apartment that still has six months left on the lease. Last week, we moved Betty in with Barron, which left her apartment available to give Brandi piece of mind

I get it, even though I don't like it.

Brandi stands up and waves, a tempered smile on her beautiful face.

I walk up and drop my bag, pulling her into my arms like a soldier coming home after a long deployment, and claiming her lips in a punishing kiss. It would be a lie to not admit I'm disappointed she isn't coming home with me—to me—but having her within a couple of miles will have to satisfy me for now.

"Hey, beautiful." I brush a lock of her blonde hair back from her face.

"Are you mad?" Brandi rests her chin against my chest and stares up at me.

I shake my head. "No. I love you too much to be mad at you. I'm disappointed that we won't be moving in together this week, but that just means I have six months to romance you and prove how perfect we are together."

"And after six months?"

"If you don't think I'm the man for you after six months—" I press my forehead to hers and take a deep breath "—then I guess I'll have to try harder."

She smiles and rubs her nose against mine. "I know you are the man for me. I love you more than I've ever loved anyone other than my daughter. But moving to a new town, a new state, is a tremendous change and after everything I went through the last time I made a big move, I need the security—"

"I know, beautiful. I get it. And while I want our forever to start tomorrow, I'm willing to take it one day at a time. Hell, I'm a happy man because you're moving to Spring City, and we can now do this right." I press my lips to her ear and lower my voice. "And it's not like I won't be tucking you into bed sated by multiple orgasms every night, regardless if it's your bed or mine."

"Let's go, crazy man." Brandi pulls back with a devilish grin, and we walk hand in hand out into the warm desert air. "I was going to take you out for Mexican food, but since you explicitly said I couldn't touch myself for the last two weeks, and are now talking about orgasms, I'm tempted to take you straight home and feed you your favorite dessert."

I drop my bag into the trunk of her Trailblazer SUV and pull her into my arms, backing her against the driver's door. Glancing around the parking garage to ensure we're alone, I slide my hand between her legs and rub circles against her mound, using the rough denim of her jean shorts to provide extra friction. "How about I get you off in the car, and at the restaurant, and then you can take me home and feed me dessert?"

Brandi arches into my hand and wraps her fingers around my biceps, her lips parted in a soft moan.

"When we're face to face, you make it very hard to say no."

"I told you the day we met—you should have a man who takes care of you physically, emotionally, spiritually, and sexually—and I am that man." I pop open the top button of her shorts and slide my hand inside her panties to find her pussy wet and ready for me.

"Oh god." She presses her face into my chest the moment the meaty pad of my middle finger finds her engorged clit primed for stimulation.

"That's my girl. You really did refrain from getting off for the last two weeks."

"Yes," she whimpers while riding my hand.

It takes less than a minute to get her off. Claiming her lips, I swallow her cries before they can ricochet off the concrete walls of the parking garage. Even though no one is looking at us, it doesn't mean they wouldn't hear her coming.

Brandi sags into my arms as I pull my hand free and suck her arousal off my fingers. "Are you good to drive?"

She looks up at me through half-lidded, sex-hazed eyes and nods. "Maybe you should drive and while I navigate."

"Whatever you want, beautiful." I walk her to the passenger side and open her door, chuckling as she squirms in her seat while buttoning her shorts. Over the last six weeks, there were a lot of late night FaceTime calls and mutual masturbation, but as soon as I booked my plane ticket to come out here, pack her up, and drive her back to Spring City, I put a moratorium on getting off for both of us. Now I have a lifetime to make her come, and plan to every chance I get.

"Are you ready to move to Colorado?" I ask from the driver's seat, my hand stretched over the console to rest on her thigh.

"I'm ready to start the next phase of my life—" Brandi brushes her fingers along my clean shaved jaw and into my hair "—with you."

The weight that's been crushing my chest since I boarded the plane this morning lifts and even though it's going to take a little longer than I would like, I know everything is going to end perfectly for us. I love her and she loves me, which means we can handle whatever else life throws at us.

"Let's go."

VETERAN
K9
TEAM
REPORTING
FOR DUTY

Second Epilogue
Brandi - Two Years later

We moved in together after Betty's lease was up in September, and Linc took a page out of Barron's book by proposing to me shortly after. He said we didn't have to rush to the altar, but he liked the idea of me wearing his ring as we built our life together.

I decided he'd waited on me long enough and suggested we elope to Vegas.

We were married three weeks later—just before Halloween—at the One Love Wedding Chapel on the north end of the Strip, and stayed at the JW Marriott west of Vegas in Summerlin for our subdued honeymoon. Betty and Barron, already married themselves, stood up for us and then had their own vacation driving back to Spring City via the Arches National Park. When we came back from Vegas, the guys at the VKC threw us a big surprise party.

Coming into Linc's military veteran world opened my eyes to a different kind of family, one not born from blood. When Betty was young, I built my social network with other young moms who worked in the hospital. As she got older, many of my acquaintances were her friend's parents, but mostly it was the two of us.

Linc maintained his Army-issued support network by moving to Colorado to work with them after separating from the military. Considering I've never been affiliated with active duty service members, I didn't understand how making that one commitment—swearing a solemn oath to support and defend—binds people in a way that only first responders and maybe communities who go through an emergency crisis understand.

These people, regardless of where they came from, are family—and now, Betty and I are part of that family. It's the support we never got but I always prayed for.

Linc pulls into the parking lot of our apartment complex as I'm walking up the sidewalk with a bag of groceries in my hand. Nowadays, I work as a CNA at the Veterans Hospital—a gig one of Linc's clients helped me get—when I'm not in class for my nursing degree. Because of all my experience, the schoolwork and practicals are fairly easy, and now that Betty is off on her own, I can afford the tuition.

"Hey Beautiful. I'm glad you're home." Linc jumps out of his car with Li-Lou.

"Oh yeah?" I smile and lift on my toes to press a kiss to his lips. "Why's that?"

"I want to talk to you about something." He grabs the grocery bag and follows me up the stairs to our second floor apartment. Setting the bag down, he quickly puts the groceries away and then spins around, pulling me into his arms with an excitement I haven't seen from him in a while.

His thinly veiled eagerness makes me giggle. "What's gotten into you?"

"What would you think about living in a big house with a couple acres where we can raise our dogs, cats, chickens, and goats?"

Shaking my head, I stare at him like he's grown a second head. "We don't have any of those things."

"Yeah, but you've talked about wanting them plenty of times." He brushes his knuckles across my cheek.

"I grew up on a small farm, that's why I talk about those things, but we can't afford all of that."

"What if we could? Would it make you happy to have all of that again, beautiful?" Linc leans his ass against the counter and pulls me into his arms. "Let's take a drive and then we'll go out to dinner."

"You're serious?" We've been looking at homes, but Spring City is expensive, and the last thing I want is to be house poor after over twenty years of pinching every penny.

"Come on." He interlaces our fingers and walks me out the door. Fifteen minutes later we're driving up a dirt road to a big log home with a forest green metal roof. It looks like the kind of house you'd find in the mountains, not out here on the plains east of Spring City. Linc stops the car outside the house and puts it in park. "You remember the retired helicopter pilot, Specter?"

"Of course, I remember Walt. We had him over for

Thanksgiving dinner last year and you have lunch with him every few weeks."

"Right. This is his property. His wife died a few years ago and his kids are scattered across the country doing their own thing, so he's out there all alone."

"Okay?"

Linc stares out the windshield for a few seconds before continuing. "I took him down to the Last Stand for a burger today. We talked for hours about our lives. He's always giving me sage, fatherly advice. Of course, I was bragging about you—how you look after long-term care patients at the VA hospital while going to school for your nursing degree."

I sit quietly, waiting for Linc to get to the point. It's rare that I see him overwhelmed—he's been supremely confident and in control since the moment he saved me on that mountain top—and I've learned to let him get there on his own. To give him some encouragement, I reach out and grab his hand, giving his fingers a gentle squeeze.

He chuckles. "I'm rambling, I know. The bottom line is, he wants to sell us this house."

Turning my eyes back to the massive tree-lined property with a barn in the distance, I shake my head. "We can't afford this."

"We can. He's practically giving it to us, if you want it."

"What? Why?"

Linc shrugs. "He said he thinks of me as family. I thought we were just two veterans bullshitting about life this last year, but after our conversation today, I realize we mean more than that to him. He wants this house, one that he built after separating from the military, to stay in the family and none of his kids want to move back here. He knows with the K9 Center expanding, we'll be here for a long time and could use a little land."

"That's very generous, but..." I bite my lip, unsure what else to say. It sounds too good to be true, which means it is.

"Before you say no, let's check out the house." Linc gets out and opens my door.

He pulls me out and holds my hand, walking us toward the front door.

"Is Walt here?"

"No. He's checking out an assisted living facility and then going to dinner."

Assisted living? Is he sick?

Saying nothing, I wait while Linc pulls a key from his pocket, and follow him into the beautiful three bedroom, three bath home. It's sparsely decorated, as if Walt had been downsizing and preparing to move out for some time. And it has a barely lived in feel, like it's waiting for someone to move in and love it.

"What do you think?" Linc pulls me into his arms while we stand on the back porch overlooking the barn and detached one bedroom cottage.

"It's beautiful, a dream, but I feel like we're taking advantage of him. I don't think I could live here."

"Yeah, I thought the same thing when he brought up the idea to me, which is why I wanted to bring you out here and show you it without him being here." Linc brushes my hair back and looks me in the eye. "How would you feel about moving in with him and providing some of his home health care? That way, we're taking care of him the same way he wants to take care of us—like family."

I frame Linc's face with my hands, only now realizing how much Walt has meant to him over the last year. "He's a surrogate father for you, huh? Why didn't you ever say anything?"

He shrugs. "I don't think I realized it until he brought up moving into assisted living. He's not ready yet, but he knows it's coming eventually, and that reality struck me hard. I've spent so much of my life alone—most of my childhood—and the idea of him dying in this big house alone tears me up."

"You are a good man, Lincoln Abrams, but from the few times I've met Walt, he doesn't strike me as the kind of man who will accept help for fear that it will be construed as weakness."

"I know. So, if you are game, we'll have to convince him. He wants to do this for us, and I want to make sure he's not alone. Both of us were abandoned by our families at young ages, and for all intents and purposes, he's been abandoned by his considering they don't want to move back to here to take care of him and he refuses to move back east."

A heavy truck door slams shut and a smoke and whiskey rasp calls through the calm air. "Where are you guys?"

"We're out back, Spec." Linc calls before pressing a kiss to my forehead. "What do you say?"

"I say we propose moving into the cottage while taking care of him in the house, having dinner together like a family, and if he agrees, we can proceed from there."

"Okay." Linc slides his hand on the middle of my back and we turn to face Walt as he opens the backdoor. To me, he looks perfectly healthy—a spry old man in his mid-eighties. But it's the smile that lights up his face when he looks at the two of us that causes my belly to tighten into knots.

"Brandi, so nice to see you again."

I walk forward and open my arms, accepting his hearty hug. "It's good to see you again, too. It's been too long."

"Ah, you work and go to school, so I try not to bother you too much." He points at Linc with a teasing grin. "This one plays with dogs all day, so I don't feel bad about pulling him away from work. So, what do you think about the house?"

We walk back inside and into the kitchen where Walt opens the refrigerator to offer us a beverage. Together, we sit in the living room with our domestic beers.

"Your home is beautiful, Walt, but we can't accept such a generous offer without making an offer ourselves." I glance at Linc who nods his agreement.

"Spec, you're in no condition to move into an assisted living facility. I mean, look at you—you're still in grizzly bear fighting shape, man." Linc smiles, using his god given charm to coax a smile out of Walt, but I see the sadness behind his eyes.

"Being mean and ornery isn't a fountain of youth, son."

Hearing him call Linc son causes the bands around my heart to tighten, especially when I see Linc's shoulders tense. He grew up with no father figure and a mother who was never home which explains why he's so attached to his Army brethren and the men and women of the VKC.

"I've been diagnosed with stage four lung cancer. I may not look or even feel sick today, but it's only a matter of time, and I want everything settled on my estate before it's too late."

Tears well up in my eyes as I see the color drain from Linc's face, and I slide my hand into his, holding him tight. "Son of a bitch. Why didn't you say anything, Spec?"

"Just found out." Walt shrugs. "Don't get all teary eyed on me, you two. I've lived a blessed life and soon I'll be reunited with my sweetheart."

"When do you start treatment?" I say softly, already thinking through all the things we'll have to do to help him through this. Doctors appointments, chemotherapy, potential surgery and recovery. He needs us more than he'll ever admit.

"No treatment, darlin'." Walt shakes his head and takes a deep draw off his beer. "I'm not spending my last days on this earth sick from a treatment that will only buy me a few more years."

"If you're not going to take treatment, then why are you moving into an assisted living facility?" I ask.

"Stay here with us." Linc says at the same time.

"You are a young married couple." Walt shakes his head. "You need your own space."

"We'll have our own space in the cottage out back. And every night we can have dinner together, catch football on the weekends, whatever you want. We won't take your generosity any other way, Spec."

I get up and move to the kitchen, opening cabinets and digging through the refrigerator without asking permission.

"What are you looking for, Brandi?" Walt asks.

"I'm going to make us dinner while we discuss this. The two of you are fairly stubborn men, so I know this will take a while." I smile and throw a wink his way. I guess after a couple of years together, some of Linc's flirtiness has rubbed off on me.

Over dinner we work out the details. Linc and I will move into the cottage over the next couple of weeks, leaving Walt in the house because one—it would be silly to move all of his stuff, and two—he should be in the same area as all the spare bedrooms for when his kids come out to visit him. He hasn't told them yet about the cancer, and I'm praying the news will get them on a plane immediately.

We moved out of our apartment a few weeks later and hosted Thanksgiving dinner at Walt's house. The entire VKC team came over to celebrate, as well as Walt's two daughters with their families. They're nice, but wrapped up in their worlds with their children, and thankful their father has us to take care of him.

Surprisingly, they aren't upset that he's selling his house for cheap to us. He set up trusts for all of his grandchildren years ago, and they're thankful he's surrounded by caring friends as the cancer progresses.

Over the last eight months we've held many celebrations until Walt was too sick to entertain guests. Today we held his celebration of life. While I've been working with the elderly for almost a decade, it never gets easier to let someone go. In a short amount of time, Walt became more of a father to us than either Linc or my real father ever were.

It just goes to show that family is formed, not born.

Betty comes over and wraps her arms around me. "You okay, Mom?"

"We'll be fine." I glance over at Linc who is saying goodbye some of his team members.

"Do you want us to stick around and help clean up?" Barron walks up and puts his big hand on my shoulder, giving me a gentle squeeze.

Glancing around the mostly clean kitchen, I shake my head. "I think we can manage the little clean up that's left."

"Okay, how about the sticking around part?" His gaze goes over to Linc and I know what he's trying to say.

Tears well up in my eyes, but it's not because Walt is gone. It's because of how unbelievably grateful I feel at this moment for our friends and family—many of which are both—surrounding us. "I'll take care of him when he's at home, you watch over him during the work day."

He chuckles and dips his chin. "Roger."

After everyone is gone, I wrap my arms around Linc and hold on to him. The two of us almost sway without saying a word, the last few weeks draining our emotions, but also filling our hearts with the outpouring of love from others.

"How about we get naked, take a hot shower, and lie in bed until we feel like ourselves again?" Linc murmurs against my temple.

"Sounds like an amazing plan." I tilt my head and press my lips to his, our kiss quickly turning passionate. Within seconds, we're clutching at each other's shirts, as if we need the physical reminder that we are very much alive. We strip each other in the middle of the kitchen, Linc's hand sliding between my legs before I can drop to my knees in front of him. Everything about this moment feels frantic, like I'll fall apart without his touch.

Linc lifts me in his arms, and I wrap my legs around his waist as he carries me back to our bedroom, the one we moved into a few months ago.

"I have to be inside you, beautiful." Linc walks through the bedroom into the bathroom, setting my ass down on the cool granite counter, burying his face in my neck as he lines his cock up to enter me.

"And I need you inside of me." I gasp as he thrusts his hips forward, my thighs spread wide and my knees held up by his forearms. Toothpaste and beauty products fly off the counter, but it doesn't matter. All the matters in this moment is me and Linc and this connection we've had since the moment he saved my life.

Just like on that first day, having him inside me reminds me I'm safe. Alive and, while in his arms, perfectly loved.

"You feel so good, beautiful. You always feel so good." Linc grunts as he comes, his arms tightening and pushing my knees closer to my shoulders. I clutch his biceps, my pussy soaked, my orgasm on the verge of releasing. Linc pulls his face back and looks me in the eye, slowing his hips to perfectly rub the head of his cock against my g-spot. "From the moment I saw you, I knew you were the one for me, and you prove me right every day that you love me."

"Every day, I love you a little more, Linc." I moan as my climax finally spills over. Linc holds himself still inside me as my pussy pulsates and my body shudders softly. When it finishes, I open my eyes and smile. "I'm so thankful you saved me that day, and every day since."

"Shower and bed?" Linc flashes a flirty smile. It's the first time he's done it in weeks, and it warms my heart, letting me know everything will be okay.

Coming next: Logan and Tess in Mine to Covet

Most of my books take place in Spring City, Colorado and feature cameo appearances from characters in past / present / and sometimes future books from all of my series. Check out my website for a cross-over / series map.

Also by Kameron Claire

Want more **Witty** Tongues, **Wicked** Needs, & **Wild** Deeds?

Hollywood Lights (Pre-Order)

* Billionaire Romance *

Show Time (Securing Selyne)

Money Shot

Three Shot

Martini Shot

Long Shot

Veteran K9 Team

* *Military Romance* *

Mine to Cherish

Mine to Crave

Mine to Possess

Mine to Adore

Mine to Covet

Mine to Worship

Mine to Protect

Mine to Treasure

Hot Nights with the Boss

** Forbidden Office / Age-Gap Romances **

Dating the Boss

Flirting with the Boss

Teasing the Boss

Tempting the Boss

Rangers Football

** Sports Romance **

Play Action Fake

Quarterback Sneak

Personal Foul

Two-Point Conversion

Red Zone

Man to Man Coverage

Short Story Collections and Bundles

Animal Attraction 4-Story Collection

Vegas Nights 4-Story Collection

Last Stand Saloon 4-Story Collection

Instalove Bundle

Grayson Enterprises Series

Bedding the Boss

Enticing the Ex

Tempting the Teacher

Wedding the Widow

Exclusives and Sneak Peeks

Get exclusive stories, updates, sneak peeks, and special content only available to subscribers...

Join our Mailing List Today!

Sign Up Here

About the Author

 USA Today Bestselling Author Kameron Claire writes stories with witty tongues, wicked needs, and wild deeds. Her books emphasize strong female leads and the protective alpha males who know how to love and support kick-ass, take-charge women. Many of her books contain military veterans, boss babes, gentle but dominant men, and goofy K9 hijinks.

Find her everywhere via linktr.ee/kameronclaire
Signed Paperbacks and discounted eBook bundles are available exclusively on her store
Subscribe to the Witty, Wicked & Wild community and read all her books online for as little as $5 a month.